HORNY TOADS

HORNY TOADS

G.W. REYNOLDS III

Rutledge Books, Inc.   Danbury, CT

This is a work of fiction. While, as in all fiction, the literary per-
ceptions and insights are based on experience, all names, charac-
ters, places and incidents are either products of the author's imag-
ination or are used fictitiously. No reference to any real person is
intended or should be inferred.

Cover artwork and illustrations by Steve Robertson

ALL RIGHTS RESERVED
Rutledge Books, Inc.
107 Mill Plain Road, Danbury, CT 06811
1-800-278-8533
www.rutledgebooks.com

Manufactured in the United States of America

Cataloging in Publication Data
Reynolds, G.W., III.

Horny Toads

ISBN: 1-58244-215-0

1. Fiction.

Library of Congress Control Number: 2002100352

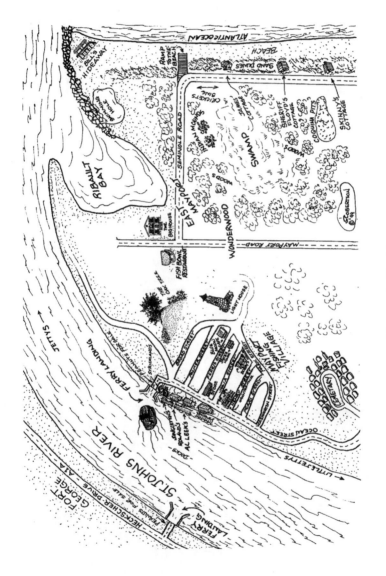

Mayport, Florida

Mayport Fleet

PRELUDE

MARGIE SAT STRAIGHT UP IN HER BED OUT OF A DEEP SLEEP. IT WAS AS if someone grabbed her and pulled her up with one motion. Even though she had been sleeping, her eyes were wide open and the words, "we want you to be the next one" echoed in her head and then faded away. She looked at the music box carousel on the nightstand next to her bed and it was no longer turning. There was no music and no colorful lights bouncing off the bedroom walls or the ceiling above her. She realized the silence had awakened her from the magic dream. The carousel dream had taken her to the sand hill and the oak tree and she had seen Mary C., Jason and Billy, the oak baby, beneath the limbs of the great tree. Margie laid her head back onto her pillow, closed her eyes, took a deep breath and thought to herself, "I know it was real. It was not a dream. I was there with them. Mary C. told me they wanted me to be next."

Margie looked at the magic music box again. She spoke her thoughts out loud. "You took me there. Your magic and the oak tree caused it all to happen." She sat up again, pushed the sheet and blanket off her body and sat up on the edge of her bed. Her eyes opened to their widest when she saw her own white sand footprints on her bedroom hardwood floor leading to the bed. Margie knew she had stood on the sand hill beneath the oak tree. She knew it was real. She knew she was next. She wanted to be next.

*   *   *

Mary C. rolled over and laid her arm across Hawk's big chest. They were both naked, as usual, after another night of marathon-level sexual relations. She had been able to keep Hawk's mind off the bizarre events of the previous day. As the dead and charred body of Eve Klim continued to smolder in the garbage drum behind the house, Mary C. made sure she and Hawk were sexually smoldering inside the house. Her explanation about the blood on the porch and the broken swing had satisfied Hawk's curiosity. Mary C. would make sure she took the trash out to the drum and did the burning until the remains of the evil Eve Klim were merely dust.

Mary C. continued to be plagued with unnatural challenges of life and death. She had once again displayed her ability to survive the evils from her past or any other evil for that matter. Within one of the more bizarre weeks in her Mayport life she had her son, Jason, return from his Giant's Motel adventure with his oak baby son, Billy. She fell in love with her newborn grandson with his mother Jessie's adult eyes, and fought for both their lives against the Mayport voodoo world, killing five in the name of all the grandmothers throughout the world.

During the same week, Mary C. faced an enemy from her past and another shotgun blast ended the evil Eve Klim's reign and hold over Sandeep Singh, the Punjabi priest. She had fortified her conviction that you can never depend on anyone else, only yourself. She found a new respect and relationship with Miss Margaret and her four daughters and thought of the young women as the sisters she never had. Mary C. missed her foolish deceased brother, Bobby, and she made French toast. Because of turmoil in her past, Mary C. knew her last few battles had been just that: battles. She also felt deep inside her soul that the war was yet to come.

Hawk turned on his side, pushed against her and put his huge arm over Mary C., engulfing her with his massive body. She liked it when he pulled her close to him. If she hadn't known better, she would have thought Hawk was having a moment of cuddling, but she would not bring that thought to his manly attention. Mary C. was like a little girl in his arms and she knew she was safe from all comers for the moment. She liked to feel safe and secure. She hadn't had such feelings too many times in her wild life. Mary C. pushed her warm body against him again and they fused together with their own body heat.

Hawk loved looking at her naked body. Any man would. Mary C.'s body had maturity and substance. She looked like a woman was supposed to look. He considered it to be a true honor and a privilege to be the man who lay with such a woman. As Hawk visually scanned her curves and bulges he had no idea Mary C. had made love to him while the dead body of her arch enemy and latest victim was burning in the garbage drum of the trash hole in the woods behind her house. Hawk would never know it and Mary C. would not think about it very often, only when she took out the trash. Her gift and ability to compartmentalize her dastardly deeds was still intact and was one of her stronger attributes. She knew the world was a much better place now that Eve Klim had been wiped from the face of the earth. Hawk would not tell her of his fight with the Punjabi priest, either. He knew when and how to keep a secret and how to burn it deep into his belly as well as Mary C. did. There is something strong and wonderful about those who are able to keep secrets within themselves.

Mary C. reached with her hand to see if their closeness had excited Hawk at all. When she touched him the hard evidence of his excitement against her hand ignited her excitement. She moved her body on top of his and straddled him as she had done many times before. It was her sexual signature. Mary C. was a true survivor, an angel of death, a grandmother and a French toast expert, but for the moment she would be a sex machine for the man who made her feel safe.

CHAPTER ONE

MARGIE STOOD IN FRONT OF THE MIRROR ON HER DRESSER AND stepped into her ragged-edged cut-off dungarees. The magic music box was on the dresser to her right. She stared at the carousel for a few seconds as she snapped and zipped up the tight denim shorts. Margie looked away from the carousel and looked back into the mirror. She put her hands on her hips and admired her small waistline. She pulled her shoulders back making her young breasts look bigger and stand at attention. She had been looking at herself in the mirror lately more than usual. A smile with straight white teeth gave her approval. There was a knock on her bedroom door, followed by the voice of her youngest and most beautiful sister, Sofia.

"Margie, you up?"

Margie adored her little sister, but didn't let Sofia know it very often. "I'm up, what is it?"

"May I come in?"

Margie grabbed her shirt off of the bed and put it on over her naked upper body.

"Of course you can come in. You are so silly sometimes."

The bedroom door opened and the young beauty with waist length blonde hair, ice blue eyes, full lips, porcelain skin, long legs, lean body and prettiest sister of them all, Sofia, walked into the bedroom. Margie looked at her little sister and realized that Sofia could very well have been the most beautiful creature on the earth. Everyone knew it. Everyone loved Sofia. Margie loved her the most.

"Why are you pounding on my door so early this morning? What do you want?"

Sofia moved past Margie and sat on the bed. "I've been thinking about all the crazy things that have been happening to us lately. Haven't you?"

"Of course I have. How can you not think about it?"

Sofia was serious."I'm scared. I know you said we're not going to be scared anymore, but I still am. I can't help it. I've tried to be brave and not think about it, but I can't help it. I'll never be good at being brave." Margie smiled as Sofia put her head down, looked at the floor and continued. "I love you so much for keeping my secrets and helping me when I don't know what to do." Sofia saw the white sand on the floor. "Look at all the sand you tracked in."

Margie's heart raced in her chest as Sofia lifted her head and Margie saw her eyes well up with tears. "I'll sweep it up in a minute. Don't you dare start crying. You'll make me cry, too. Now, stop it, right now." Sofia stood up, stepped to Margie and hugged her. "I said stop it," Margie said, but returned Sofia's emotional hug. Margie ended the tender moment with her extremely dramatic little sister. "I'm going to see Miss Mary C. today. You want to go with me?" Sofia's big blue eyes popped open.

"I don't think I do! Have you forgotten what happened the last time we went over there together?" Margie smiled.

"I haven't forgotten any of it. I think about it all the time. In fact, it was the wildest thing I have ever been involved in. It was exciting and dangerous. And guess what? It didn't hurt us now, did it? Nothing happened to us. We survived it all. I'm going back over there." Sofia would not leave it at that.

"A man got shot in front of us. Miss Mary C. shot him with us standing right there. Then the voodoo woman held the baby up into the air and everyone went crazy. Then all those people died that night. No thank you. I'm not going back there." Sofia noticed the carousel on the dresser. "We have to give that back to Jason, you know? We shouldn't keep it here. It scares me, too. I'm at the point where everything scares me. You said we weren't going to be scared of things and I went in the opposite direction. I'm scared of more things than ever before."

Margie had to smile at Sofia's dramatics and lengthy true confession. "Sofia, you are so funny." Sofia's eyes were still wide open.

"I'm not trying to be funny at all. I'm trying to tell you how scared I am and you think I'm funny."

Margie smiled. She knew she was about to add to Sofia's stress but she had to tell Sofia what she had done. "I used the carousel again last night." Sofia's eyes were wide open again.

"Margie, are you crazy? Why did you do that? Do you want something bad to happen to you? Please stop using it for those dreams." Margie was serious, too.

"I told you I'm not going to be scared any more. I want to know about these kinds of things. Remember, we talked about how we know nothing of life outside of our mother. We have been so sheltered and I feel like a sponge just soaking up all I don't know. Don't you want to be brave like Mary C.? At first, I was thinking maybe we needed to stay clear of her, but the carousel has changed my mind about that."

Sofia shook her beautiful head. "Listen to yourself, will you? 'The carousel changed your mind?' Do you hear how strange that sounds? You act like it's alive."

Margie smiled and shrugged her shoulders. "I'm going to see her, with or without you. I don't need you to go with me."

*   *   *

The police investigator, Mr. Butler, and Officer Jimmy Johnston sat on a couch in the emergency room of the Beaches Hospital, waiting for Sandeep Singh, the Punjabi priest, saint, warrior and former slave, to get his broken jaw set and wired back together. Mr. Butler was tired and disgusted.

"I don't think we can hold him on anything. He ain't done nothin' wrong that we can prove. The Mercedes is registered in his name. He says he fell on the dock and broke his jaw. Havin' your hair all chopped up ain't no crime."

Jimmy Johnston could see Mr. Butler's struggle with the strange foreigner who had come to Mayport. "You still think he was the one who helped Mary C. the other night, don't ya?" Mr. Butler nodded.

"I'd bet my pension on it. Remember, it came out of her mouth. She called him Singin' Sandy. His damn name is Sandeep Singh. That's close enough for me. It all fits together. It always seems to fit when that woman's involved. In a matter of days we've had a man shot by Mary C. in her front yard, but no complaint from the victim. Then, that same night the same man was killed at Mary C.'s house along with three other Mayport men and Mayport's own voodoo queen. And let's not forget the Werewolf girl being split opened like a butchered chicken while she just happened to be running through the woods on a night with a full moon in the sky." Mr. Butler stopped talking for a few seconds. Jimmy didn't respond. He knew Mr. Butler had more to say. "Now something has happened to this Sandeep character. And I don't think he's the kinda man that's gonna walk away from bein' done wrong. And I don't think the black folks in Mayport are gonna lose four of their men and the voodoo queen without doin' something about it. You mark my words. None of this is over. At least that crazy bunch of circus folks are gone. That's why I went ahead and gave them that wolf girl's body. There was nothin' we could do and it got them out of town. It was an accident and no sense chargin' them boys in no killin'. It's over, but there's more comin'. You mark my words. Plenty more's comin'." For some reason Mr. Butler changed the subject. "You still takin' all those youngin's to that damn Gator Farm in St. Augustine this Sunday?"

Jimmy was surprised with the question, but he answered it. "Yes sir, I'm hopin' to get a few more adults to go with me. You interested?" Mr. Butler looked at Jimmy.

"Not hardly. I ain't goin' nowhere with little children, especially them bad actin' children in that group of yours. I don't know how you do it. I always want to put 'em in jail." Jimmy smiled at Mr. Butler's rare moment of humor.

Mary C. left Hawk in the bed so he could have time to recover from the effects of unleashing her sexual mo-jo. She loved draining him of his strength, stamina and body fluids. Mary C.'s grandmotherly instincts moved her to Jason's bedroom where she pushed open the door and looked into the room. She heard the toilet flush down the hall so she knew Jason was up and about. Mary C. moved to the zinc galvanized number ten washtub lined with blankets next to Jason's bed and smiled when she looked into the tub and saw her grandson, Billy, with his big green eyes opened wide. The baby smiled back at Mary C. as if he recognized his grandmother and her heart raced in her chest as the fine hairs stood up on her arms and neck.

"Mama, you all right?" Mary C. knew Jason had joined her and the child, but she didn't turn around to greet him.

"I'm good, son. I feel much better this morning. It's like I've been able to do away with some ol' bad feelin's and memories." Jason smiled and moved closer to his mother and his son.

"I'm sorry 'bout me not bein' here to help you, Mama. I can't stop thinkin' 'bout what you went through. I feel ashamed."

Mary C. touched Billy's little face and responded to Jason without turning to face him. "I've got strange feelin's about what happened. I'm not mad at anybody. I did feel alone and I will probably feel that way again. I've learned you can't depend on anyone but yourself. I just didn't expect to have such a strong and hard lesson." Mary C. turned to face Jason for the first time. She had to be Mary C. "And you should feel ashamed."

*   *   *

Mr. Butler looked up to see two of his police officers, David Boos and Paul Short, walk into the small waiting room of the Beaches Hospital. Officer Jimmy Johnston stood up to greet his fellow policemen.

"Y'all get anything from him?"

David Boos shook his head. "The man hasn't said one word to us. Or anyone else for that matter. He's got a broken jaw and it's a pretty bad one. His hair's been cut all up. I'd be willin' to bet somebody really kicked his ass."

Mr. Butler stood up. "I need to talk to him. Show me where he is."

Paul Short nodded his head. "They're setting his jaw, now, sir."

Mr. Butler stopped moving toward the door. "I still don't think we can hold him. He's done nothin' wrong that we know of. He's pretty strange to begin with and we can't prove he's connected to any crime. Bein' strange ain't no crime. I still want to talk to him, though. Take me to him."

*   *   *

Margie was downstairs in the kitchen. Her mother, Miss Margaret, was at the stove.

"I'm going to visit Miss Mary C. for a little while, if that's all right?"

Miss Margaret turned to her oldest daughter. "Aren't you working today?"

"Yes ma'am, but later. I'll relieve Sofia later today. Sofia's going with me. Then she'll go to work." Sofia entered the kitchen as her oldest sister made her declaration.

"I'm going where?" Margie turned to Sofia and smiled.

"We're going over to see Miss Mary C. and Billy, remember?"

Miss Margaret spoke up before Sofia had a chance to express her protest as she had done in the bedroom a few minutes earlier. "You girls are so good to folks. I am so proud of my girls and the way they think of others. I'm sure Mary C. will love having you two stop by. She does love you four girls. It's like you girls are the sisters she didn't have." Sofia glared at Margie. She knew she could not back out of the visit and she could not openly make a protest. Miss Margaret took a deep breath and gave the two girls a strange warning.

"Ya'll be careful. The last time you two went to visit Mary C.

it got pretty exciting around there. If anything seems strange get on back home."

Even the brave new Margie didn't like her mother's warning. Sofia's beautiful blue eyes were wide open as she gave Margie another stare and glare. Margie smiled again as if to say, "We're going. Sorry about mother's warning."

*   *   *

Mary C. stood on her front porch holding her oak baby grandson, Billy, in her arms. Hawk walked out of the house and looked toward the damaged porch swing Mary C. had destroyed with her shotgun attack on her enemy, Eve Klim.

"Damn, Mary C., I forgot about the swing. You really blew that critter and the swing all to hell, didn't ya?"

Mary C. smiled. "Straight to hell."

Hawk stepped to Mary C. "I don't think it's worth fixin'. I'll just buy you a new one."

Mary C. smiled again. "Now, that's the way a woman should be treated. New things. I like new things." She kissed Hawk as he moved past her and the baby. The kiss ended when Jason blew the truck horn and they both looked up.

"Hey, you two. Quit smoochin' in front of the baby and let's go fix that winch. We gotta catch some shrimp. Daylight's burnin'."

Mary C. smiled. "Listen to him, this mornin'. Worryin' about catchin' shrimp." She looked back at Hawk.

"What's wrong with the winch?" Hawk moved down the three porch steps.

"It's jammed up, but I can fix it. We're goin' out as soon as I fix it."

Mary C. nodded. She had no idea Sandeep Singh's hair was the reason the winch was jammed. But, by the same token,

Hawk didn't know Mary C. had killed Eve and burned her body in the garbage drum in the woods behind the house. Mary C. had a little whisper for her man as he moved away.

"Remember, you gotta wench right here at home could always use a little fixin'." Hawk shook his head at his over-sexed partner and her aggressive style and joined Jason in the truck. Mary C. waved to her two men as Jason drove the truck out of the front yard.

The master shrimper, Earl Todd Singleton, called Chichemo after his shrimp boat of the same name, had left Hawk and Jason to shrimp on their own. Chichemo's lessons had ended and he had taken his boat and his monkey, Bosco, to try the waters off the coast of Fort Myers, Florida in the Gulf of Mexico. Hawk and Jason were not experienced enough to leave Mayport to explore far away shrimping grounds. They would remain local shrimpers as long as they remained shrimpers at all.

* * *

Mr. Butler pulled the green curtain back in one of the small hospital emergency room cubicles. The Punjabi priest, Sandeep Singh, was lying on one of the beds. The warrior-priest had his eyes closed. His face was swollen from the broken jaw. The Punjabi had one side of the bed covered with what was left of his eight foot long hair. His hair on the other side of his head had been unevenly chopped up and was a greasy mess. Mr. Butler had to talk to him.

"Mister, you awake? I really need to talk to you." Sandeep opened his eyes. "I'm sorry to bother you, you bein' hurt and all, but I'd like to know what happened to you and ask you a few other questions." Sandeep spoke, but his jaw had been wired shut and he was only able to move his lips.

"Have I done something wrong?" Sandeep's teeth remained clinched together as he talked. He made a sucking sound after every three or four words. "You are the law here. You must think I have broken your laws."

Mr. Butler stepped closer to the side of the bed. Sandeep closed his eyes again. It was obvious he was in great pain. Mr. Butler was determined.

"I need to know what happened to you. How you got hurt? Who cut your hair like this?"

Sandeep made the sucking sound, opened his eyes and took a deep breath. "The forces of evil have met in your town and the strongest still stands and has set me free from my bondage." Mr. Butler looked at the three officers standing with him in the small room. Sandeep continued. "I have shamed and disgraced my ancestors and the holy Kirpan. I must reclaim the holy sword and protect all who are golden."

Mr. Butler didn't understand but he wasn't going to allow the strange priest to stop talking. "I hope ya get to do all that stuff, but how'd you break your jaw and what happened to your hair?" Sandeep made the sucking sound again before he spoke.

"The evil deed of blood forced upon me was not needed because the true devil was burning. I was punished because I chose the wrong road to freedom. I did not know the angel of death would repay me by giving me my freedom."

Mr. Butler looked at Jimmy Johnston. "Why do I feel like I know the angel of death he's talkin' about?" Jimmy didn't respond as Sandeep raised his head up off of the pillow and had more to say.

"The Kirpan must be reclaimed. I cannot live with such shame." Sandeep laid his head back down on the pillow and closed his eyes once again.

Mr. Butler raised his eyebrows as he looked around at the three officers. "I knew she'd be involved. It never fails. He thinks she did something to repay him for helping her that night."

Sandeep opened his eyes. "She is not golden. The child is. Her son could be golden again, but he is fading."

Mr. Butler moved even closer to the bed. "I don't know what the hell you're talkin' about, Mister, but I need to know what's goin' on and what's gonna happen next. I got a real bad feelin' you know the answer to both those questions." Mr. Butler was surprised with Sandeep's response.

"I will tell you whatever you ask of me. I am Punjabi. I am a priest and holy man."

Mr. Butler took a deep breath. "Yeah, that may be true, but you're a little more than a priest, don't ya think?"

Sandeep's teeth stayed closed as his lips moved. "I am many things, but I am a priest first."

Officer Paul Short joined the conversation. "And as a priest you'll tell us the truth?"

"Of course. I have no reason to lie to you. Perhaps the truth will be my penance."

Mr. Butler didn't care how painful it was for the Punjabi priest to talk. The investigator was ready with a barrage of questions.

"Were you the only one with Mary C. the night of the killins?"

"I was there. She did not see me."

"Why did you go there?"

"I went to see the child. He is golden."

The three officers and Mr. Butler were all ears. "What makes you say the child is golden? What does that mean?"

"He is more than all of us; one of a kind. He may be the

most golden the world has seen. I do not know why he is in this place, but my destiny was to come here so I would know the child existed."

Mr. Butler did not care about the mystical golden child subject. "You killed those men for her?"

"They were after the child. I could not allow that to happen. I am a protector. My pledge is to defend the weak. It was my destiny and my duty. I will always protect the golden."

"You killed them all?"

"No. I had to kill three."

Mr. Butler looked at the three officers. "Three for the priest and two for the angel of death. It gets better all the time. And ya know what, fellas? We can't do anything about it. They were defending themselves against a group of invaders who were there to kill them. Our local black widow doesn't even know he was there. She thinks she killed them all by herself." Mr. Butler looked back at Sandeep. "Since you're bein' all truthful and everything, what happened to you, anyway?"

"To gain my freedom, I was to kill another."

The police force in the room was all ears again. Mr. Butler had another question. "Gain your freedom? Who had taken it from you?"

"My soul mate. The one with the black heart."

Officer Jimmy Johnston knew what the Punjabi priest meant. "The woman with you? You needed your freedom from her?"

"Yes."

Mr. Butler wanted his first question answered. "Who broke your jaw and cut your hair?" Sandeep took a deep breath as if he was considering not answering the question. Mr. Butler wanted more. "You been doin' real good up to now, mister. You need to keep talkin'."

Sandeep made the sucking sound with his mouth again. "I

was to kill the one they call Hawk to gain my freedom. God walked with him, not me."

Mr. Butler couldn't help but look at Jimmy Johnston and give him a half smile. Mr. Butler had to speak his mind. "I've heard the one called Hawk, as you say, don't die so easy." The three officers smiled at Mr. Butler's remark. Sandeep nodded his head.

"Yes, I would say that is true."

Officer David Boos had to join the questioning. "You went to kill Hawk 'cause she told you to do it?"

"Yes, and I was punished for my sin."

"Where's the woman, now?" It was all ears time again after Officer Boos' important question.

Sandeep did not hesitate with his answer. "She is gone. Her black heart is no more."

Mr. Butler took the lead again. "Please tell me she just left town."

Sandeep made the sucking sound and swallowed. "She just left town."

* * *

Mary C. turned toward the front door of her house when she heard someone knocking. She could see two figures on the porch, but couldn't see who was calling through the curtain on her new door. She pulled the curtain open and saw Margie, the oldest sister, and Sofia, the youngest, standing on her porch. Mary C. smiled and opened the door.

"Oh, my goodness! Look at you two, visiting me again so soon. What are y'all doin' out and about this early?"

Margie took the lead as usual. "Hey, Miss Mary C. I had to talk to you and Sofia wanted to say 'hey' too. And we miss seeing Billy."

"Well, come on in girls. He's wide awake in here. He'll be glad to see you, too. Hawk and Jason went down to the dock to do something to the winch on the boat. Always somethin' breakin' down on these damn shrimp boats." Margie walked into the front room of Mary C.'s house. The oak baby, Billy, was lying on his stomach in the middle of a big thick quilt on the hardwood floor. Sofia got on the quilt with him. Margie looked at Mary C.

"Miss Mary C., can I talk to you privately?" Sofia looked up at Margie. Mary C. looked at her, too.

"Why sure you can. Come on out on the porch. Sofia can watch Billy while we talk." Sofia was surprised and didn't like it, but she gave a half smile and turned to the baby on the quilt. Margie knew Sofia wasn't happy about her private audience with Mary C., but Margie didn't care. She was on a mission. Margie and Mary C. walked back out onto the front porch. Margie looked at the broken swing.

"Oh, Miss Mary C., your pretty swing is broken to pieces. What happened?"

Mary C. pulled the chairs together. "Silly me. I was scared of this big fat raccoon that crawled up there. I think it was sick. It was in the swing and so I shot it. I didn't think about hittin' the swing when I pulled the trigger. I was just scared it was goin' to bite the baby. I killed the 'coon and the swing at the same time." Mary C. smiled at her little joke.

Margie was too excited for chitchat. She took a deep breath and took over the conversation. She got right to the point. "Miss Mary C. I'm honored you want me to be the next one, but I'm really scared about having the next oak baby. I thought I was ready to do it, but I'm not too sure if I can go through with it."

Mary C.'s face changed and Margie saw her puzzled look.

"Margie, what are you talkin' about? Are you with child, girl? Who got you pregnant?" Mary C. was a three-question woman, but it wasn't the three questions Margie was looking for. Margie knew she was right.

"It's all right Miss Mary C. When you told me you wanted me to be the next one, I was honored. I just needed to talk to you about it. Get some of your courage." Mary C. stared at Margie as she continued. "You don't have to pretend with me. Your secret is safe. I just need to talk to you about what you want me to do. I hope I can do it for you and Jason."

Mary C. had to speak up. "Now listen to me, little missy. I'm sure you ain't been drinkin' this early so I know you ain't drunk. I do think you've had a dream of some kind and you think it was real."

Margie smiled. "Of course it was real. And you know you're right about the dream. It was a magic dream. You know, from the tree and the music box. The magic carousel sent me to the tree to be with you. I'm not scared of the magic box any more."

Mary C.'s eyes were wide open due to Margie's strange and fast talk. "You gotta slow down, child. Stop and let me catch my breath while you do the same. You ain't makin' much sense, but I do think you are serious about what you're sayin'."

Margie tried to change to a slower gear, but it was difficult with the degree of excitement she had inside her. "O.K., I'm sorry. I want to be the next one, but I'm still a little scared. I'm not like you and I need to find more courage. I'm doing much better, but I still have a long way to go. I've been babied and sheltered all of my life. I just can't be brave all of a sudden. I just came over to tell you not to give up on me. I will be the next one."

Mary C. still had a puzzled look on her face. "Margie, what is it you think I want you to do?"

"I know what you want. It's all right. Just help me. I want to do it."

"Margie, do what?"

Margie felt Mary C. was testing her and she was ready. "I know you have to be careful. I know this is a very delicate situation. If the only time we can talk is during the magic dreams, I'll wait for the next one. If I made a mistake in coming here, I'm very sorry. I'll wait until you call me, but no matter what you say or don't say, I understand."

The screen door opened and Sofia walked out onto the porch holding Billy. "We don't want to stay inside. We want to be with you two out here in the fresh air." Mary C. and Margie turned to Sofia and the child. Mary C. smiled.

"Well, come on out here with us." Sofia walked to Mary C. and sat down in the third chair. Sofia knew her presence had ended the private conversation, but like Margie, she didn't care. Margie would wait for another opportunity to continue the conversation with Mary C.

*   *   *

Mr. Butler and Officer Jimmy Johnston stood next to a police car in the parking lot of the Beaches Hospital. Officer David Boos was at the wheel of the car and Officer Paul Short was his passenger and partner. Mr. Butler stepped to the car.

"David, I've got to get back to the station. Jimmy's gonna go out to Mayport and question a few more people about all this craziness. You and Paul see where our new friend goes when he leaves here. I guess we want that Mercedes to drive right on out of town, but I don't think that's gonna happen. Let me know if he goes back to Mayport. I've got a feelin' somebody's gonna pay for his broken jaw and bad haircut."

* * *

Mary C. and Margie sat in the porch chairs. Sofia was standing and she handed Billy to Mary C. "I've got to relieve Peggy at the store in ten minutes. I wish I could stay longer, but work is calling me and I'm sure Peggy is too."

Margie smiled. "Sofia, you are so funny sometimes."

"You girls are always workin'. I think it's wonderful how y'all take care of that store like ya do."

Margie responded. "Only because we have to. Not because we want to."

Sofia walked down the porch steps. "Margie, don't forget you relieve me at three."

Margie smiled. "Don't worry, I'll be there." Sofia rolled her big, beautiful ice-blue eyes. She had heard that empty promise many times before. She knew Margie was not very dependable as the relief person at the store. Margie couldn't wait for Sofia to move on out of the yard and on up the road. Mary C. turned to Margie. It was time to continue their strange conversation. Mary C. was as anxious as Margie.

"What was you carryin' on so about before Sofia came out here?"

Margie was ready. "I saw you and Jason and Billy at the tree, this morning. I know what you want of me. I want to do it. I'm just scared. I came here to say that."

"You saw me at the tree?"

Margie nodded her head. "All three of you."

"And I asked you to do somethin'?"

"You told me you wanted me to be next."

"Next for what?"

"Next to have an oak baby."

Mary C.'s eyes and face lit up. "Girl, I was wrong. You have been drinkin'."

"No ma'am, I haven't been drinking. It was real and I know it was. I know the magic music box took me to you in a dream, but it was a real dream. They're dreams, but real, too."

The words 'magic music box' rang in Mary C.'s head. "Hold on a minute! Back up for me, please. Did you say the magic music box took you to me?"

Margie nodded. "Yes ma'am. You know the one you and Jason use to call people to the tree: the merry-go-round. Oh, you know what it's called, the carousel. That's it. The carousel.

Mary C. adjusted Billy in her arms. "You have a carousel music box that you think belongs to me and Jason?"

"Jason told Sofia it came from the circus people, but I know that's not true. You had it all along. He just can't tell her. I think he thought Sofia was the one, but I knew it would be me."

Mary C. wanted to know more and she knew Margie, the oldest of the sisters, was ready to tell all she knew. "Where is the music box, now?"

"Sofia's keeping it in her room for Jason. Well, actually it's in my room right now, but she's the one he asked to keep it for him. I didn't understand that at first, but now I know it was really so I would use it to come to you at the tree. I consider this an honor. I'm just nervous about it, that's all." Mary C.'s puzzled look was gone. She would listen to Margie and find out all she could.

CHAPTER TWO

MR. JOHN KING, THE OWNER OF THE HAUNTED HOUSE IN MAYPORT, stood next to an open grave in the town of Gibsonton, Florida. He watched a wooden casket as it was lowered into the deep hole. The belly dancer, Ana Kara, held his arm and also watched the casket going down. Mr. King looked across to the other side of the grave where Big Bob, the giant, and Norman Bates, the skeleton man, stood with their heads bowed. Ming and Ling, the Siamese twins, sat on a stool to his left. Black Beulla, Tom Thumb, and Helga were standing near the twins. Big Bob would conduct the private and simple ceremony.

"We have already said many things about how we feel about Beth and her untimely death. We have been sad, mad and confused. No one will make fun of her or be scared of her where she is now."

* * *

Officer Jimmy Johnston's patrol car was headed toward Mayport, Florida. He was going to the fishing village to investigate the Punjabi priest's situation. Jimmy also wanted to see if his wild sex partner, Margie, was working at the store. He was hoping to find her and indulge in her sexual favors. He visualized her in the back of the store bending over one of the tables with him standing behind her. It had become one of their favorite positions and Margie liked the excitement and danger of doing it in the back of the store while she was supposed to be minding the front counter. Jimmy's manliness pushed against the front of his pants. It was a great vision as his police car passed the little jetties.

*   *   *

Margie had completed her story about the magic music box Jason had given to Sofia for safekeeping. Mary C. let Margie talk until she had told all she knew and her wild experiences with the carousel, including her dream with her sister, Sofia, when they were in the same sex dream at the tree. Mary C. had gotten excited when Margie told the sex parts. Mary C. took the next step.

"Margie, I want you to bring the carousel to me. Can you do that?"

Margie smiled. "Of course I can. It should be with you. You don't need to use it on me anymore. I'll go get it right now."

Mary C. nodded and smiled. "Thank you Margie. Now, hurry!"

Margie was up on her feet and off the porch. "I'll be right back."

*   *   *

Officer Jimmy Johnston stopped his police car in front of Miss Margaret's store. He was hoping Margie was working, but he knew if she wasn't, he could find out where she was. Sofia was there to relieve Peggy, but Peggy hadn't left yet. The two sisters saw the police car pull up out front. Peggy had to comment.

"Well, here comes Margie's law man. She says he's got two big sticks."

Sofia turned to her vulgar sister. "You stop talking like that. He's nice. He'll hear you."

Peggy had more to ruffle Sofia's feathers. "Yeah, Margie calls one a night stick and the other a fright stick."

Sofia's eyes lit up. "I said to stop that. He's coming in." Peggy smiled as the bell on the front door sounded and Officer "big stick" Jimmy Johnston entered the store. Peggy couldn't help herself. She forgot to use the official Miss Margaret store greeting.

"She's not here. She works later today."

Sofia cut her big eyes at her rude and crude sister. "Is that how we are supposed to greet our customers?" Sofia turned to Jimmy. "Good morning, Officer Johnston. May I help you with something?"

Peggy shook her head. "Jimmy, isn't she the most adorable thing you have ever seen? Sofia, you are a riot. Or as mother would say 'you're a hoot'." Peggy looked at Jimmy. "Sorry, Jimmy. I was just playing with you and being silly with Sofia. This place makes you silly every now and then."

Jimmy smiled. "Silly's good, sometimes."

Peggy smiled back at him. "Now, that's a strange statement coming from you, don't you think?"

Her comment got Jimmy's full attention. "Why is that?"

Peggy was ready with her sarcastic answer. "Well, Margie says you are never silly. You're serious all the time. You act older than your age."

Sofia was once again appalled at Peggy's brazen comment. "Peggy, you stop talking about personal things Margie discusses with you."

Peggy kept looking at Jimmy, but she talked to Sofia. "He

knows he's not ever silly. Why does me saying it make a difference?"

Jimmy took a deep breath. "Peggy's right, Sofia. I've tried to be a little silly now and then, but it never feels right for me. I guess I've been grown up too long, maybe too early. Margie's helping me to be a little more relaxed about things. Maybe I'll be a little silly one day. Who knows? Please tell Margie I'll stop by later."

Sofia felt bad and had to say something to him. "Margie's visiting Miss Mary C. She might still be there."

Jimmy nodded and smiled after the information. "Mornin', ladies." The bell on the front door rang as Jimmy left.

Sofia was outraged with Peggy. "What's wrong with you? I can't believe how rude you were to him."

Peggy didn't care. "He comes here to have his way with our crazy oak tree loving sister. I don't think he's ever bought a pack of gum."

Sofia was ready to defend Officer Jimmy Johnston. "He buys stuff all the time. Maybe he just doesn't buy things from people who are rude to him, like you." The bell on the door rang again. The two sisters turned to see Jimmy step back into the store.

"Oh, by the way, I came to invite all of you to go to St. Augustine with me on Sunday. I'm takin' my scouts to the Gator Farm and maybe to the old fort if we have time. I need a few more adult eyes to watch over that interesting group of mine. I think it will be fun. You're welcome to go if you'd like to. Maybe I'll act a little silly." Peggy smiled at Jimmy's moment of his own sarcasm. "The bus will leave right after church. If you're there, I'll know you're goin'. See y'all."

Peggy looked at Sofia. "He just wants us there to take care of those wild boys he's always taking places. I'm not going anywhere and babysit those little demons."

Sofia was still disgusted with her sister. "You are so mean lately. Every time Jimmy's around you are so mean to him. Are you jealous of him and Margie?"

Peggy was surprised at Sofia's question. "Oh, ha, ha! You bet."

"Well, something's wrong. I just might go help him with those boys on Sunday. It might be fun to get away for the day."

"I'm sure you will." Peggy changed the subject. "I wonder where your secret admirer, the priest, and that awful woman are today? Are they still here?"

Sofia was surprised with Peggy's question. "How would I know?"

Peggy had more. "Well, Mr. King's house looked empty when I went past there this morning. It was all closed up. No cars out front and the circus bus was gone. Doesn't that seem just a little strange to you?"

"I didn't look that way when I came in. I was thinking about Margie and how badly she wanted to see Miss Mary C. this morning. They had a private conversation."

Peggy's eyes lit up. "Well, you do know our older sister has gone a bit dopey lately, don't you?" Sofia nodded her head. She had to agree.

*   *   *

Jason and Hawk stood next to the winch on the shrimp boat, Mary C. Jason saw that the rotating wheels were clogged with clumps of jet-black hair. Jason looked at Hawk.

"That looks like hair."

Hawk nodded. "It is."

"Where did it come from?"

"That Indian fella stayin' at the King house. It got caught in the wheel. I cut him loose."

"Can we get it out?"

"I think so. If I turn it on and go slow, we can pull in one direction while the wheel turns the other way. I hope that'll do it. It'll take us both to do it."

Jason wanted to know more. "He was here on the boat?"

Hawk nodded. "He came here to kill me."

Jason's eyes popped open. "Why?"

"He said something about killin' me would set him free from somethin'. It sounded like a religious thing. I didn't really care why he was here. I just didn't want to die."

"You fought with him?"

Hawk nodded and smiled a strange smile. "Yeah. Me and a few friends. I took his knife."

Jason was concerned. "You think he'll come back?"

"I know he will. It ain't just a knife. It means somethin' to him. A man don't need to keep souvenirs from his victories over other men. I already took his hair. Now, I've got his prized possession. Oh, he'll be back all right."

"Where is it?"

"It's in that ol' rusty tackle box on the back porch at the house. I tossed it in there to hide it, I guess. I guess I wanted a trophy. I wish I hadn't done that, now."

Jason was curious. "What if he does come back for it? He might try to kill you again."

"I'm sure he will."

* * *

Mary C. looked out the window of her house and saw Margie walking up to the front porch. Margie was carrying something wrapped in a towel. Mary C. met her at the screen door.

"That was fast. You must'a ran all the way home like that little piggy did." Margie smiled at Mary C.'s nursery rhyme humor and walked up the three steps to the porch. Mary C. held the screen door open as Margie entered the house. Margie moved to the living room and sat down on the couch, placing the covered carousel on the small coffee table in front of the couch.

Mary C. sat down next to Margie and Margie unwrapped the magic music box. Mary C.'s eyes flashed when the beauty of the antique carousel was revealed as Margie removed the towel. Mary C. was speechless.

"This is the magic music box Jason left with Sofia." Mary C.'s heart raced and her eyes sparkled. "Isn't it the most beautiful thing?"

Mary C. smiled and found her words. "It is truly beautiful. And this belongs to Jason?"

"Yes, ma'am it does. He said it came from those circus people. They gave it to him when he left them to come home. It sent me to the oak tree to meet with you. I thought you knew about what it does."

Mary C's eyes widened again. "What it does? What do you mean?"

Margie gave Mary C. a strange look. "Are you telling me you don't know anything about this thing?"

"I'm sorry to disappoint you, Margie, but I have no idea what it does."

Margie smiled. "You have to say that to me because you are obligated to the secrecy of the tree, right? You can't reveal to me what you know unless we're at the tree, like last night."

Mary C. smiled. "I wish I could help you with all this stuff you're dealing with, but I'm not the one. Now, what exactly does this thing do? You said it made you dream beautiful dreams. Then it scared you. Then it took you to the tree to see me. How does it do these things?"

Margie was more than ready to talk again, now that the carousel was actually there with them. "I think it's better when you're alone. Sofia and I did it together and had a real scary dream. When I was alone it was better." Mary C. touched the carousel as Margie continued. "You turn it on and it plays music, it turns and lights flash off the walls. It makes you relax and sleep. It's a wonderful feeling. I think when it stops you wake up. It seems that way."

Mary C. was more than interested. "What if we just turned it on right now? What do think would happen?"

Margie didn't know the answer. "I'm not sure. I have a feeling it would just play and spin with no magic. I don't think it does it all the time."

"You think it would be all right to turn it on so we can see it turn and hear the music?"

"I don't see why not." Margie reached out her hand and pushed the small switch that turned it on with her finger. The miniature horses of the carousel began to turn and the music began to play. A hundred colored lights began to bounce off the walls of Mary C.'s living room. Mary C. smiled with delight at Margie as the lights danced in both their eyes. They laughed out loud as the lights covered the walls and ceiling of the room. They looked down at the carousel as it began to spin faster and saw nothing but the colored lights.

Mary C. looked up and she was alone in her bed. She was naked and on her back staring at the ceiling above her. The lights were bouncing off the walls. She lifted her head to see a group of men standing in the room. She looked at each face and knew them all. Some of them were from her younger days and some were from encounters of her later years. Mary C. thought she saw Sheriff Floyd standing in the corner of the room behind the others. She thought she saw James Thorn holding a bottle of Jack Daniels whiskey. She thought she saw Charlie Klim in the crowd, but when she looked again he was not there. She felt no fear at all as a strange warmth took over her naked body. The men came closer to the bed and began touching her.

Hands rubbed her legs and arms. She was wet and her nipples hardened. Lips touched her, too. She lifted her arms over her head as she had done many times before during moments of pleasure. Mary C. opened her legs as she saw the tops of men's heads moving up and down her thighs and between her legs. She felt her body fluids rising from her toes and flowing through her body until she exploded and for the first time in her sexual life Mary C. actually screamed with ecstasy and sexual pain. She opened her eyes. There were no lights around her. The music was silent. She touched herself and felt warmth and wetness. Mary C. sat up and realized she was naked in her bed. She thought of Margie and the music box. She wrapped the sheet from her bed around her body, stood up and walked to her living room. Margie was not there. Mary C. saw her clothes and Margie's clothes on the hard wood floor.

"Margie, where are you?" Mary C. looked at the music box. "Margie!" Mary C. walked down the hall. "Margie!" She looked into Jason's bedroom and her eyes widened when she saw Margie, spreadeagle and naked in Jason's bed. She moved to the bed and pulled the sheet up, covering Margie's body. Mary C. had been properly introduced to the magic carousel.

* * *

Officers David Boos and Paul Short watched the Punjabi priest and warrior, Sandeep Singh, walk across the hospital parking lot and get into the front seat of his white Mercedes

Benz. They watched for a few seconds. Then the car moved away. They would follow Mr. Butler's request and see where the strange man was going.

*   *   *

Sandeep's hair was no longer tangled in the winch of the shrimp boat. Hawk held up a handful of the black shiny hair. "You think I should save this for him? He might want it back." Jason looked at the clump of hair.

"I don't think he's comin' back."

Hawk smiled. "Oh, he's comin' back, all right. It won't be for the hair, but he's comin'."

Jason didn't like Hawk's response. "Why ya think he's comin'?"

"Men like him don't take to losin' too good. I was lucky this time. I don't know if I would be able to handle him by myself. I shouldn't have taken the knife from him. I just wanted to do somethin' else to him so I took his knife."

Jason was enthralled with Hawk's words. "And you think he'll come for the knife?"

Hawk nodded and took a deep breath. "Count on it."

Sandeep Singh parked his white Mercedes in front of Bob's Barber Shop at the end of Seminole Road in Atlantic Beach, Florida. A police car stopped across the street on the side of Ace Lanagan's gas station. Officers David Boos and Paul Short watched from their surveillance position as the Punjabi priest stepped out of his car and entered the small barbershop. Even with his injury and his thought of retrieving the Kirpan, his disciplined mind was alert enough to realize he was being followed.

All eyes in the barbershop looked up at Sandeep when he walked into the shop. The talk in the room ended when they realized a stranger with a broken jaw and seriously damaged hair had joined them. Everyone in the room stared at the big man with hair down to the floor on one side of his body. All four barber chairs were full and there was another customer waiting in the row of chairs along the window. Bob, the shop owner, greeted the strange new customer.

"Be right with ya, sir. Have a seat." Sandeep nodded and sat down in one of the empty chairs. "We got coffee and donuts from Cinotti's on the table, if you're hungry. You look like you could use a pick-me-up."

Sandeep moved his lips. "Thank you, but I do not need anyone to pick me up. I want someone to cut my hair off."

One of the barbers, Walter, joined in. "Looks like somebody started cuttin' and then stopped. That's a bad lookin' jaw ya got there, fella. Makes me hurt just lookin' at it. You ain't from around here are ya, boy?"

The third barber, Jim, was curious, too. "Where ya from, mister? I know it sure as hell ain't from around here."

Sandeep's teeth remained clinched tight as his lips moved. "I am from far away. I am Punjabi. I am a priest."

Walter's eyes lit up. "I'm a man of God too, mister. I'm Southern Baptist." Sandeep respectfully bowed to Walter. Walter had more questions. "Pan-Jabby, that's over near Nahunta in Georgia, ain't it?"

Sandeep shook his head. "I do not know of this place called Nahunta."

Walter shrugged his shoulders. "It don't matter none."

The fourth barber was a woman, Lynda. She spelled it with a "y". Sandeep liked her blonde hair and her athletic build. Lynda only stared at the stranger for a few seconds and continued cutting her customer's hair. She tried not to look at the Punjabi, but it was hard for her not to. Bob pulled the striped sheet off of his customer.

"There ya go, Justin. That should hold ya for a while." The young man paid Bob. Bob turned to Sandeep. "You're next, Mr. Pan-Jabby." Sandeep looked at Bob. The other barbers smiled.

"I am Punjabi." Sandeep looked at Lynda. "Sandeep will wait for the woman. She will have the honor of cutting my hair." The three male barbers and the customers all looked at Lynda when the stranger made his choice. Walter couldn't help it.

"She always thinks it's an honor to cut her customer's hair." Lynda cut her eyes at Walter. She was finishing with her customer and Sandeep would be next. Lynda was nervous when Sandeep stood up from the chair he was sitting in and stepped to her barber's chair.

*   *   *

Mary C. and Margie were both dressed and sitting on the couch in the living room. Mary C. looked at the carousel. "What the hell happened here? Are you all right?"

Margie was dazed from her daytime sexual encounter with the music box. She looked at Mary C. "I didn't know it would work during the day."

Mary C. was in mild shock, too. "Well, I don't know what it did to you, but I can tell you it did something to me. And even though I didn't like some parts of the dream, it was pretty good for me. I ain't never let go like that. Dream or not."

Margie was ready to tell about her daytime dream. "My dream took me to the oak tree again. Jason was there with me. I think it was real. I can still feel him inside me."

Mary C. had to stop Margie's moment of true dream confession. "Damn, girl! Don't tell me about my son still bein' inside ya. I don't want to hear that."

Margie looked down. "I'm sorry. I thought you wanted to know what happened to me."

Mary C. smiled. "When Jason gets home we're gonna have to have a talk about this dream maker."

Margie was amazed at Mary C.'s attitude toward what had just happened. "Doesn't anything scare you?"

"Lots of things scare me, Margie, but havin' all those men pleasure me in a dream sure ain't one of 'em."

*　*　*

Hawk stopped his truck at the front of Miss Margaret's store. Jason jumped out of the passenger's side door and went into the store. The bell over the front door rang as he pushed the door open. Sofia turned from her work at the shelves to see her true love walk into the store. Her beautiful face lit up like a candle. "Jason! Oh my goodness! How are you?"

Jason did love the way Sofia talked. "I'm fine. And you?"

"Oh! I'm fine, too, now that I've seen you. May I help you with something?" Jason knew Sofia would greet him with the proper and official Miss Margaret greeting. It just took her a little while to present it that time.

"Hawk's thirsty for a orange Nehi and I'm cravin' a strawberry."

Sofia smiled and moved to the cold drink icebox. "Isn't it funny how you can crave something and you just have to have it or you will surely die from the wanting?" Jason smiled at Sofia's dramatic words as she reached into the icebox and pulled the two colorful drinks out of the icy water. She held them up to Jason. "These are really cold. They should do the trick. Don't drink it too fast or you'll get a headache." The icy cold water dripped off both the bottles as Sofia handed them to

Jason. As Jason took the bottles from her, she kissed him on the lips. Jason didn't move. He loved the tender moment.

"I've missed you." Jason smiled and moved to the cash register counter. He knew Hawk was waiting in the truck. Sofia stepped behind the counter.

"When can we spend some time together?"

Jason knew he didn't have time to talk to her. "We've got to take some nets to the dock for Mr. Leek. Then, we're goin' home for a little while before we go shrimpin'. Hawk's waitin' in the truck. I really need to go."

"I visited your mother this morning." Jason was surprised. "I saw Billy. I held him again. He's so beautiful." Hawk blew the truck horn. Jason handed Sofia the money for the two Nehi drinks.

"I gotta go."

*   *   *

Mary C. and Margie were sitting on the front porch when Officer Jimmy Johnston drove his police car into Mary C.'s front yard. The two women were recovering from their sexual dream encounter with the magic carousel. Mary C. had her grandson lying on his thick quilt on the floor of the porch at her feet. Officer Jimmy Johnston stepped out of his car and walked toward the porch steps. Mary C. greeted him.

"Well, well. It's Officer Jimmy Johnston come to visit. My cup runs over with company today." She looked at Margie. "I don't think you're here lookin' for me." Jimmy smiled and walked up the porch steps. He nodded to Mary C.

"Mary C." He looked at Margie. "Margie." Margie smiled and had to tease her serious friend.

"Ain't you the silver-tongued conversationalist this mornin'? What brings you out here?"

"I'm lookin' for you.

"Well, here I am." Mary C. looked at Jimmy. Jimmy looked at the damaged swing. It was torn to pieces.

"What happened to your swing?"

Mary C. knew the perfect answer. She had given it before. "I had to kill a sick 'coon. He crawled up into the swing and I was scared it would hurt the baby. When I shot it, I didn't think about tearin' up the swing. I just blew it all to hell."
Mary C. was more than ready to change the subject. "So, Officer Johnston, what does bring you out this way on this fine Mayport mornin'?"

Jimmy looked at Margie again. "Well, I was lookin' for some adults who might want to help me on an outing with my scouts Sunday after church. I'm takin' 'em to the Gator Farm in St. Augustine. It'll be fun and educational for us all. I need all the adult eyes I can get to watch those little rascals. You two wouldn't be interested, would ya?"

Mary C. looked at Margie. "I ain't been to that Gator Farm in years. I only been there once. You ever been there?"

Margie shook her head. "Never." Jimmy gave a half smile.

"The entire day will be on me. I'll take care of the transportation, tickets and food. What'a ya say?"

* * *

Lynda put the sheet over Sandeep's body and fastened it around his neck. She could see where the tattoos stopped on his neck. On one side of his body his hair hung down to the floor, covering the side of the chair. On the other side his hair was cut off close to his shoulders and there were uneven and jagged cuts in the back. Lynda was nervous. All eyes were on her and her unusual customer. Lynda had to ask the normal barber's question.

"How would you like it cut, sir?" The room was silent except for Lynda's deep nervous breathing. It might have been her nerves, but it could have been something else. Sandeep Singh was a big, strong, handsome man.

"Cut it all off, please. Shave it clean. The punishment must be complete. It will be at your beautiful hands." Lynda looked at the other three barbers. They were all grinning like orang-utans. Sandeep had more. "I will not carry my crown of honor again until I have reclaimed the holy Kirpan and atoned for my great sins."

Jim looked at Walter. "Ain't this where you need to jump in?"

Walter looked at Sandeep. "I don't think so." Lynda took out her scissors first. She went to work on the Punjabi priest's hair.

CHAPTER THREE

OFFICER JIMMY JOHNSTON SAT ON THE TOP PORCH STEP. MARY C. sat in one of the porch chairs with Billy in her lap. Margie sat in one of the other chairs. Jimmy was also there on police business.

"Miss Mary C., you heard any talk about that Indian man who's been stayin' at the King house? Or that strange woman with him?" His question surprised Mary C., but she did not change her facial expression. Mary C. would give no indication she knew all about the strange woman and her timely death. She was the master.

"What kind'a talk? Folks been talkin' about them since the day they hit town. Not to mention all those carnie people."

"Well, the circus people are gone. One of them got killed and they went back home."

Margie's eyes widened at Jimmy's unexpected information. "Killed? Who got killed?" Mary C.'s eyes widened too, waiting for Jimmy's answer.

"It was a woman. She wasn't with the group stayin' at Mr. King's. She got killed in the woods off Seminole Road. Some young men were bow huntin'. They thought she was an animal. They shot her with a huntin' arrow."

Margie was shocked. "They thought she was an animal?"

Jimmy nodded. "They thought she was a wild wolf." Mary C. and Margie looked at each other. Margie couldn't believe what he said. "They thought she was a wolf?"

"Yeah. She was the Werewolf Girl in the circus. And was she ugly. She really looked like a wolf. She had a wolf's face and hair all over her body. She even howled at the full moon."

Mary C. joined in. "And they thought she was a real wolf runnin' in the woods? They killed her?"

"Yes, ma'am. It's sad, but it was a hunting accident. Those circus folks were real torn up over it. It was pretty clear they had strong feelin's for the young woman."

"That's awful." Margie was mad. "She comes to Mayport and now she's dead. We've got more people dying around here." Margie didn't think about Mary C.'s recent encounter with five dead Mayport citizens. Again, Mary C. didn't change her facial expression. Margie looked at Mary C. and realized that Mary C. had been the cause of some of the deaths she was talking about.

"Oh, Miss Mary C. I am so sorry I said that. I didn't mean it about you." Mary C. smiled.

"You worry too much, girl." Mary C. looked at Jimmy.

"Why ya askin' about that Indian man?"

"'Cause somethin' happened to him. Somebody beat the fire out of him. They broke his jaw and cut off some of his hair. I just saw him in the hospital. He says he's lost somethin' and I think he's comin' to Mayport to find it. And the woman's gone, period. The Indian says she left town. It's all pretty strange though. She left town, but he still has the car. It's all strange, don't ya think?"

* * *

Lynda, the barber, had the biggest pile of hair she had ever cut on the floor at her feet. She had lathered up Sandeep's head with shaving cream and was slowly dragging her straight razor across his head. In a few more seconds there would be no evidence of his eight feet of raven black hair he had carried throughout his entire Punjabi life. It was like it never existed. All other activities in the shop had stopped. All eyes in the building were glued to Lynda and the warrior priest. Lynda guided the razor's blade over his head one last time, taking away the remains of the lather. Bob, the owner of the shop, couldn't resist.

"Damn son, you look like Uncle Festus from the Addams Family."

Sandeep nodded his new bald head. "It is a good thing to look like the uncle of this family?" Everyone in the shop nodded their heads. Bob responded for them all.

"Yeah, sure. It's good to look like Uncle Festus."

* * *

Officer Jimmy Johnston stood next to his police car. Margie stood with him. Mary C. was on the front porch with Billy. Jimmy smiled at Mary C. and then turned and whispered to Margie.

"I can't believe she wants to go with us to the Gator Farm." Margie whispered back to him. "Well, you asked her."

"I know I asked her, but I didn't think she would go."

Margie smiled. "Well, go on back up there and tell her you were just being nice and she can't go."

"Oh, very funny. Mr. Butler's gonna have a fit if he finds out."

Margie didn't understand. "Why would he care what you did on your day off on your own time?"

"He would care, trust me. I always get myself into these things. And she might even bring the baby. Why would she take the baby? He's an infant. The little thing won't even know he's there. This is crazy. I gotta stop bein' so nice to people. I gotta think before I talk."

Margie smiled at Jimmy's frustration. "I'll talk her into leaving the baby with Mother. Calm down. Like you said, 'It will be fun for us all.' You wanted help. You got it."

Mary C. sat with Billy in her lap while Margie and Jimmy talked at the car. She knew they were lovers because she had walked in on them having sex in Margie's bedroom. Mary C.'s thoughts gave her that vision of Jimmy in full tumescence, standing behind Margie. Mary C. smiled. It was one of her many favorite sexual positions. Jimmy kissed Margie good-bye and got into his police car. Margie walked back and joined Mary C. on the porch.

"That Jimmy's a good young man, ain't he?"

Margie nodded. "Yeah, everybody likes Jimmy."

Mary C. raised her eyebrow. "I think you like him the most. Remember, I saw proof of how much you like him with my own eyes." Margie looked down. She was embarrassed by the reminder. "I know. I was so embarrassed and ashamed that day. No telling what you thought of me."

Mary C. smiled. "I thought you were young and exciting. It made me hot inside. I liked it." Mary C. changed the subject. "What about the music box? This ain't no toy."

"No, ma'am, it's not. It scares me sometimes, but I can't quit thinking about it."

Mary C. understood. "I can see why. I ain't sure what happened earlier, but I know I liked it. And the way you ended up in that bed, naked and all, I think maybe you liked it too." Margie put her head down. Mary C. had a suggestion.

"Leave it here with me. It's time to talk to Jason about it."

Margie nodded. "Yes, ma'am."

*   *   *

Lynda, the only lady barber at Bob's shop, finished shaving the back of Sandeep Singh's neck. She wiped off the last spot of white lather and splashed the usual barbershop cologne after-shave on his neck and the side of his face. Sandeep's lips moved.

"That is a very pleasant fragrance. Thank you. What is the cost of your service?" Lynda took off the hair-covered sheet that covered Sandeep's body.

"You're welcome, sir. That'll be two dollars, please." The three other barbers and the customers looked at the pile of black hair on the floor next to Lynda's chair. The spectators were quiet as Sandeep took a roll of paper money out of a pouch strapped to his ankle and handed Lynda the fee. He looked into the full-length wall mirror at his new look and his self-afflicted penance. He turned to Lynda.

"Your touch was confident and sure. You are a woman of substance in a man's world. Thank you for allowing me to share in your talents."

Lynda looked at her fellow barbers and the customers. "Thank you." Then she looked at her unusual customer. She didn't know what to say. Sandeep bowed to her and left the shop. Bob looked at Lynda.

"He didn't pay you in puka shells, did he?" They all laughed as Bob moved to the window. "He's drivin' a white Mercedes. You don't buy those with puka shells." They all moved to the window as the Punjabi drove away. A police car pulled out of the gas station across the street from the shop and followed the Mercedes.

*   *   *

The sound of the Platters singing "Magic Touch" came from the jukebox in the Blue Moon Tavern. Four black men and the black woman called Macadoo sat at a table near the back corner of the room. They were all listening to one of the older men.

"This thing's bad, I tell ya. This cannot go unchallenged. Something has to be done." Macadoo nodded her big head.

"What do we do?" The man continued.

"We have lost four of our best young men and one of the respected elders. I didn't care for Voo Swar's voodoo nonsense, but I respected her for her convictions and her dedication to her beliefs."

Another man joined the conversation. "But the fact still remains they went there to kill that woman and take the child. How they all died remains a mystery, but they were the thieves in the night."

A third man spoke angrily. "That devil woman had already shot Truck and she didn't care who she hurt. She never has."

"Well, they still went there to kill her and that's not right no matter what you say."

Macadoo nodded again. "Ol' Voo Swar must'a really believed the child was worth killin' over. I felt the child's power, but I don't know why Voo Swar would have wanted to take the child at all. Something moved her to react so quickly. Perhaps no one will be able to use his powers. They say there was another force that night. Voo Swar and the others thought they were taking hell to the woman, when in reality, she took hell to them. I want her punished, too. But I don't want to be the next one to die at her hand."

The older man spoke again. "The law will say she was

defending herself and the child. It will be over and she will continue her evil ways. There are always dogs to protect the devil. Hers come in many forms. I also know our brothers and our sister met the woman's forces of evil. They were not prepared for the likes of what they met that night. No human, black or white, would have been prepared for the evil at her house that night. We'd all be smart to leave it alone, but I know we can't."

* * *

The white Mercedes Benz passed Silver's Bar and the Jamboree Club at the beginning of Mayport Road. The pleasant aroma of the Milligan hamburgers cooking next to Silver's touched Sandeep's nose. He was going back to the Mayport village to find the holy Kirpan sword he had lost to the man called Hawk, better known to his mother as Lester Hawkins. From what they thought was a suitable distance behind, officers David Boos and Paul Short followed the Mercedes in their police car. Paul had Mr. Butler on the police radio.

"You were right, sir. He's headed back to Mayport. Bald head and all. He's keeping the speed limit, but he's definitely going back." Mr. Butler hesitated before he answered. "You there, sir?"

"I'm here. He's bald-headed?"

"Like a baby's butt, sir."

"Stay on him. I got a bad feelin' about this. Be careful. He don't look it with that broken jaw, but he's a bad man. I think Jimmy's over there somewhere. I tried to get him on the radio, but no answer. I'll try again and tell him y'all are headed that way. Use him as back up if you need him. Over."

Officer Jimmy Johnston stopped his police car near the steps at Mr. Leek's fish house as Hawk and Jason walked out of the main double doors.

"Hawk, Jason. Can you talk to me for a second?"

Hawk and Jason stopped. Hawk answered the question. "We're hurryin' home so we can get a few things. The boat's ready to go. What can we do for ya, if it don't take too long?"

Jimmy nodded. "Just a minute, please.

"Shoot."

"Do y'all know anything about that Indian fella that's stayin' over at the King house?"

Hawk didn't react to the question and had his own question. "Like what?"

"Well, for one thing, do ya know what happened to him? He's got a broken jaw, his hair's been cut up and he says he's lost something. And that woman who was with him is gone. Y'all seen anything suspicious?"

Hawk shook his head. "The damn place has been crawlin' with circus people, this Indian shows up in a white Mercedes with a mysterious woman, five people die at the house, and I'm sure the ghosts are runnin' wild at the King place and you are askin' us if we've seen anything suspicious? Hell, Jimmy, what ain't suspicious?" Hawk nodded and walked past Jimmy.

"Sorry I held y'all up."

                              *   *   *

Mary C. stood on her back porch and looked out toward the wooded area behind her house. She could not see the garbage hole, but she knew it was there. She could not see the garbage burning drum either, but she knew it was there. She could not see the burned remains of Eve Klim, but she knew they were there, too. Mary C. considered walking out to the drum to see what remained of the awful woman she had killed and burned. The thought did enter her mind to see if any bones were left in the drum that might have to be taken out and buried in the woods. She knew Jason often burned the trash and he would eventually see the bones. She decided to look later.

Mary C. was barefoot and when she stepped back toward the door she stepped on the flat top of a nail that had worked its way up and out of the wooden board of the porch floor. She lifted her foot quickly and grimaced in pain.

"Damn, that hurt." She lifted her foot to inspect the damage. The flat top of the nail had left a mark on her foot, but did not penetrate or cut her skin. Mary C. looked down and saw the nail. She looked around on the porch for a hammer or something to drive the top of the nail back into the board. She saw nothing that would do the job. The rusty metal tackle box on the porch floor caught her eye and she bent down, opened the top of the box, looking for a tool of some kind to assist her with the nail. Mary C. only saw hooks, corks, bobbers and fishing line. She reached in and lifted the top tray exposing a deeper section of the box. Her eyes widened when she saw a large, beautifully crafted knife with a viciously angled half moon curved blade lying in the bottom of the box. She reached in and took the knife out of the box. Mary C. had no idea she was holding the holy Kirpan that belonged to Sandeep Singh, the Punjabi priest. It was also the blade that assisted her the night the Calypsos came for the oak baby. It did cut fast, clean and deep.

* * *

The white Mercedes stopped in front of Miss Margaret's store. Sofia was minding the store and she looked out the front window when the luxury car stopped. She knew it was the car that Sandeep drove for the mysterious lady, Eve. Sofia was excited about seeing the Punjabi priest, but she wasn't pleased with the thought of having to talk to the evil woman. At first she didn't recognize the shaved headed Sandeep as he stepped out of the car. It only took her a few seconds to see it was her admirer with his long mane of hair gone. Sofia covered her mouth with her hand as he walked into the store and she recognized him. She could also tell he was injured. She was truly concerned.

"Oh, Mr. Sandeep! What has happened to you?"

Sandeep bowed to the young woman he considered golden. His teeth remained clenched as only his lips moved when he talked. "I am being punished for my sins against the one they call Hawk."

Sofia didn't really hear his words. "What happened to your hair?"

"I had it removed as part of my penance. I do not deserve to wear such adornments."

"Your face is swollen and bruised. Are you in very much pain? It looks painful."

"That is part of my penance, as well."

Sofia was sad about her strange friend's pain and appearance. "Please, come sit with me. Can I get you something to drink? Are you hungry?" Sandeep bowed his head in respect, made the sucking sound and moved his lips.

"Eating will be difficult for me. My jaw has been broken."

Sofia closed her eyes at the thought of the broken jaw. "Perhaps a drink of water?" Sofia opened her eyes. "You sit down and rest for a while." Sofia turned and moved to the back of the store, leaving Sandeep alone in the front of the store. He did not sit down. He moved to the front window and watched a truck passing on the road. His heart pounded in his Punjabi chest when he saw the man called Hawk driving the truck. Sofia's voice interrupted the moment.

"Here you go." Sandeep turned to see Sofia standing there

with a tall glass of water with a long paper drinking straw sticking out of the top of the glass. Sandeep stepped to Sofia and took the glass in his hand. He touched the paper straw and looked at Sofia. He stirred the water with the straw. Sofia smiled.

"I thought you might need to use a straw to drink it. It's a straw. You suck water through it into your mouth." Sandeep put his lips on the straw and looked up at Sofia. She smiled. "Just suck on it." He followed her directions. Sofia smiled when she saw water moving through the paper straw and into his mouth as he pressed his lips and sucked.

"That's it. I hope that makes it feel better."

Sandeep took the straw from his mouth. "Yes, it does. Thank you. I was very thirsty." He sucked on the straw again.

"You probably won't be able to eat any regular solid food for a while. Just soft things." Sandeep looked at Sofia's big ice-blue eyes and did not respond. Sofia didn't care. She really wasn't looking for a comment. She was just talking. "I've never seen anyone with a broken jaw. It makes me quiver inside."

"You are kind and you feel for others. That is part of what you are." Sofia hadn't talked to the priest very much lately, but she liked the way he talked to her. It was flattering and uplifting. It made her feel special and different. The Punjabi talked to her like she was an adult and had something to offer the world. She liked that. Sofia had questions for the priest.

"Where did everybody go? Mr. King's house looks empty and it was full of people two days ago. And now, it really looks like a ghost house."

Sandeep nodded his head. "I don't know where they have gone. The last time I saw some of them they were defending their fellow man. They were the true warriors against evil. I do not know where they have gone. I wish I could see the two who are one. They are a gift to the world. We are better when they are near."

Sofia's eyes lit up. "You mean the twins, don't you? They are so beautiful."

"Yes, you call them twins. Yes, the twins are beautiful and much more."

"I love the way you talk. I've never heard anyone talk like you." The bell on the door sounded. Sofia and Sandeep turned to the door to see Mr. Leek walk into the store. It was obvious to Sofia that Sandeep's presence in the store surprised Mr. Leek. She greeted him with the official Miss Margaret store greeting.

"Good morning, Mr. Leek. May I help you with something?"

Mr. Leek looked at Sandeep. "My God, it's you. What happened to you, son? I didn't recognize who you were at first with your head shaved like that and all. You really look different. And it looks like you've broken your jaw. I've seen one or two in my time. I am sorry."

Sandeep bowed to Mr. Leek. "Thank you. I know your concern is sincere. It has been clear to me you are a man of substance. I will be fine. I am Punjabi. I will survive."

Mr. Leek nodded his head. "I have no doubt about that, son. Y'all getting' ready to leave?" Sofia looked at Sandeep. It was a good question.

"Yes. My companion has already gone. I will follow soon."

"You still stayin' at the King house?"

"No. They have gone."

Sofia had to ask. "Mr. Leek, don't you think it's strange how the King house is empty? They're all gone."

Mr. Leek knew the answer. "They left this mornin'. Mr. King went with them."

"Is he coming back?"

"He'll be back. He took one of them back in his hearse." Sandeep lifted his head and Sofia's eyes opened wide.

"In his hearse?"

"Yeah. One of their friends got killed in the woods. It was an accident. They took her back home. They were here to find her in the first place. It was very sad. John is a good man. He took the body back for them. He really likes those people."

Sofia's eyes were still wide open. "Who got killed?"

"None of us saw her. Her name was Beth. She was the Werewolf Girl from the circus. Some young men hunting with bows thought she was a wild animal and they shot her."

"That's awful. How could they think she was an animal?"

"They say she looked like a wolf—hairy, yellow eyes, wolf teeth, howled at the moon. All that kinda' stuff."

Sofia's face showed her disgust and astonishment. "She howled at the moon?" Sofia's eyes were their biggest. Sandeep looked at Mr. Leek and joined the conversation.

"There are many strange things in our world. I have heard of such creatures, human, but with some animal features. They usually do not make themselves known to the world and they live a hermit's life, hidden away. They are tormented by normal unfeeling men, who are afraid of the unknown."

Mr. Leek had more information about the Werewolf Girl. "Mr. King said the tall man told him she had come here to breed with Jason. She heard the stories about the oak tree and wanted him to help her continue her species." Sofia's eyes were opened even wider than her widest.

"She wanted what?" Sofia looked at Mr. Leek.

"She thought she was the last of her kind and she considered Jason as the one to help her have a child to continue her breed. She's the reason the circus people came here. They wanted to find her and take her home before she did something stupid. They were too late." Sofia thought of Beth's yellow eyes when the Werewolf Girl had stood over her at the oak tree when she was preparing to make love with Jason. She would never tell the fact she had seen the half-animal woman first-hand and in the flesh. Mr. Leek took a ball of net twine off one of the shelves.

"I need to fix my son's cast net. He hooked it on something sharp and tore a big hole on one side."

Sofia stepped behind the counter and opened the cash register. "You want this on your bill, Mr. Leek?"

Mr. Leek shook his head. "No, little lady, my tab's all clean here. I'll pay cash as I go. How much?"

"Sixty cents." Mr. Leek gave Sofia a dollar. He looked at Sandeep as Sofia gave him his change. Mr. Leek didn't like the Punjabi priest being in the store with the young, beautiful and impressionable Sofia.

"When ya think you'll be headed out of town so ya can catch up with Eve?"

"Soon."

"Yeah, ya said that. What does that mean? Soon today, tomorrow? Soon, next week?" Sandeep bowed his head to Mr. Leek the interrogator.

"Just soon." Sandeep turned to Sofia and gave another bow. He walked to the door and pushed it open, ringing the bell. Then he turned back to Sofia.

"I hope to see you and say good-bye before I go. Thank you for all your kindness." Mr. Leek looked at Sofia as Sandeep left the store.

* * *

Mary C. opened the front door as Hawk reached for the

doorknob. It surprised him as the door moved from his reach. He was eye to eye with his woman.

"Damn, you scared me, woman. I 'bout fell on my face."

"Sorry. I've been waiting on y'all."

Hawk walked into the house, followed by Jason. "I wasn't sure if you was comin' back before ya went out or ya would just leave from the dock when ya fixed the winch. I take it you got it fixed?"

Jason finally spoke up. "She's ready to go. We just came home for a few things and to say good-bye."

Mary C. had a sarcastic moment. "Now, how sweet was that. Y'all comin' home to say good-by and all." Hawk looked at Mary C. as she moved past him and into the living room. Jason picked Billy up off the quilt on the floor. Mary C. turned to Hawk.

"Maybe y'all came back for these." Mary C. stood next to her coffee table in front of the couch. Jason turned to see what his mother was referring to. His eyes widened when he saw the carousel he had given to Sofia for safekeeping on the table. He looked at his mother.

"How did that get here?"

"You tell me. It belongs to you."

"It was gift a from Big Bob when I left there."

"You asked that girl to keep such a thing for you? You didn't want me to see it, did you?"

Jason knew his mother was right, but he would never admit it. "It's not just a music box. I was going to tell you about it when things calmed down. It does strange things."

"No shit, Sherlock. I've already seen what it can do." Jason put Billy back on the quilt. Jason didn't like it when his mother used profanity or was sarcastic. Hawk entered the room. He saw the carousel. He didn't know what was going on.

"Look at this thing. It must be an antique." Hawk moved closer and his eyes widened when he saw the Kirpan sword Mary C. had placed on the table next to the carousel. Mary C. knew Hawk saw the sword.

"Here's something you might need." Mary C. picked up the sword and held it out to Hawk. She couldn't help herself. "You boys got all kind'a goodies here, don't ya?" Hawk took the sword from Mary C.'s hand. She was still in her sarcastic mood. "Let's see, here now. We got a merry-go-round music box, that I might add, is magic." She looked at Hawk. "And, we also have this damn big fancy knife that looks like it can cut your head off. Where exactly, did these things come from?" Jason looked at Hawk. Hawk looked at Mary C.

"I took the knife off that long-haired Indian. He was gonna cut my head off with it and I just couldn't let him do that. He was busted up pretty bad when he left. I guess I kept the blade as part of the ass whippin'."

Mary C. seemed satisfied with Hawk's explanation. She even seemed pleased with what he said.

"You really kicked that man's ass?" Hawk didn't respond. "They said he's some kind'a soldier, a trained fighter. I wonder why he wanted to kill you? You are the damnedest man I've ever seen. My man's a butt kickin' man." Hawk looked down. He didn't like Mary C.'s tone, but he knew she was pushed with the situation at hand. He was trying to make up for the fact she was alone when the voodoo woman and the Calypsos came calling. He would not challenge her about her annoying attitude. She looked back at Jason. Jason knew he would have to explain the carousel. Mary C. had her own question before he could give his explanation.

"What would possess you to give this beautiful thing to that child to keep for you? Why did you do that? It seems so strange to me, but there's lots of strange things goin' on around here. What could that child do with such a thing?"

Jason couldn't say he didn't want his mother to have it because he knew she would use and abuse it once she learned what it did. He was right.

"She thought it was beautiful and I let her keep it for awhile. I was gonna get it back. I just didn't think about it with all the other things goin' on around here."

Mary C. smiled and seemed to take his weak reasoning in good spirits.

"Those pretty young girls will take a man's attention away, won't they?"

"Yes ma'am. I 'spose so."

Mary C. looked at Hawk and then she looked back at the carousel. "Wait 'til you see this thing in action."

Jason pressed his lips together. "Mama, please be careful with it."

Hawk didn't understand. "What are y'all talkin' about? What does it do?"

Mary C. was ready. "It makes you dream; wild colorful dreams."

"Ain't no music box gonna make you dream. Maybe the music relaxes you enough to make you sleep, but it ain't magic."

Mary C. smiled and changed the subject. "What ya gonna do with this big ugly knife?" Hawk held the holy Kirpan up in front of his face.

"I don't know. I guess I could bone some shad with it. It looks like a good bonin' knife, but I never got your brother, Bobby, to teach me how to do it. You know he was the only man I knew could bone a shad?" Mary C. nodded. Hawk continued. "I could cut some buds with it. I ain't cut no buds since

I was a boy. It looks like it could really be a good bud cuttin' knife."

Jason was curious. "What's a bud?"

Mary C. had to be Mary C. "My God, son, have you been so sheltered?"

Jason looked puzzled, but Hawk rescued him. "Buds are the middle stem growin' out of a small palmetto palm bush. You usually use a machete to cut 'em. The buds are used by the Catholic churches on Palm Sunday. When I was a boy we would cut the buds and sell them to the priests in the area. The priests bless the palm strips and give them to the congregation. This here knife would be good for cuttin' buds and killin' rattlers. You always run into big rattlers when you're cuttin' buds. They like layin' under them fans."

Mary C. changed the subject again. "You shrimpin' on Sunday?"

Hawk wasn't sure about Mary C.'s question. It did come out of the blue.

"Of course we're shrimpin'. Gotta go when they're runnin'. You told me that when I first started shrimpin'. Why? Did you think I might not go? Is there a reason you want me to stay home?"

"No, you're right. You gotta go when they're out there. I told Margie I'd go to St. Augustine with her and Jimmy on Sunday. I thought you might go, too, if you didn't go out shrimpin'."

Hawk was still puzzled. "St. Augustine? What y'all gonna do there? Go to the ol' Spanish fort?"

"Actually, if we have time we're gonna go there, but we're goin' with Jimmy Johnston and his scouts to the Gator Farm first."

Hawk's eyes lit up like floodlights. "You mean to tell me

you're goin' to see those nasty hard lucks?"

Shrimpers considered alligators to be bad luck. Even to say the word, alligator, was thought to bring on the bad times. No Mayport shrimper talked about the hard lucks.

Mary C. shook her head. "Now, don't tell me that Lester 'Hawk' Hawkins, the ass whippin' man of Mayport, has that stupid shrimper's superstition about alligators. Hell, you ain't been shrimpin' long enough for that. Bobby drove me crazy with that silly stuff and now you're takin' over for him."

Jason joined in. "Nobody could say that word around Uncle Bobby. He would really get mad and sometimes he would just leave wherever he was. You couldn't say it. If anything went wrong that day he'd blame the person who said that word."

Hawk's eyes were wide open and still lit up. " Ya see, Mary C. It ain't good to say it. Please don't say it. Don't play around like that. Ain't no reason to use that word if you don't have to. And how long I've been shrimpin' has nothin' to do with the way I feel about them hard lucks." Mary C. shook her head and realized Hawk didn't want to play with her about the word, 'alligator.'

"You're serious, ain't ya?"

"I sure am. I hate that word. Even before I started shrimpin' I hated that word."

"You do sound like Bobby. Like Jason said, Bobby didn't want anyone to say it. He'd really get mad at me. He'd have a damn fit. And if anything went wrong the day I said it, he'd blame me all day. It ain't a word ya say too often, ya know?"

"That's true, so it don't have to be said at all."

"I never thought you would be that way about anything. I wonder why it came to be a bad luck superstition? It had to start somewhere."

"Let's don't talk about it, please. I just think it's bad luck; always have. I guess it came from my father. He told me it was bad luck and his daddy probably told him. You get taught somethin' when you're little and it has a tendency to stay with ya, that's all. Can we drop it?" Mary C. knew Hawk was serious and she didn't continue, but Hawk did. "Why would you want to go there and see them nasty things anyway? That word will be written on signs all over the place."

"Just to do somethin' different. Get away from Mayport. I like bein' with those girls. They make me laugh. I can help Jimmy keep an eye on those bad little boys he's always foolin' with. Maybe I need to do a good deed. Margie's gonna ask her mama to keep Billy for the day. I was gonna take him, but he's too little to enjoy it."

Hawk was still concerned. "Can't Jimmy take the boys somewhere else? How 'bout the ol' fort? Does it have to be that awful place? I don't like this Mary C. I don't say much to you about things like this, but I don't like this at all."

"You can't think like that, Hawk. You ponder on somethin' in your mind and it is sure to happen. Folks speak the words sometimes and they come true. It's better not to say things sometimes. It's like tellin' somebody to be careful or they'll get hurt and sure enough, you speak the words and they get hurt. It happens all the time. The less said sometimes, the better off things are." Hawk was disgusted with her long and worthless rationale.

"I can't help it. Messin' with them damn hard lucks won't bring nothin' but misery to somebody. I just hope it ain't us." Hawk took a deep breath. "Do what you want. You usually do, don't ya?"

"Well, I guess this means you ain't goin' with us, huh?" Hawk looked at Mary C. She had a big smile on her face. Hawk had to smile, too.

"Are you always gonna get your way and do what you want?"

"Probably."

Jason picked Billy up off the floor and took him to his bedroom. Jason put the baby on the bed and laid down next to him. The conversation in the front room was over.

"Jason, let's go. We need to be out past the jetties within the hour." Jason placed a pillow next to Billy so he would not fall off the bed. He walked out onto the porch. Hawk was getting into the truck and Mary C. was standing on the ground at the driver's side window. Jason got into the passenger side of the truck.

"I'll see y'all in the mornin'. Be careful and catch a mess of them hoppers, will ya?"

Hawk had a serious look on his face. "You gonna be all right?" Mary C. touched his arm.

"What do you think?"

Hawk shook his head.

Mary C. looked across the cab of the truck at Jason.

"Take somethin' so ya don't get sea sick."

"Yes ma'am."

CHAPTER FOUR

THE HUGE BLACK WOMAN, MACADOO, SAT AT THE CORNER TABLE IN the Blue Moon Tavern. Only two men sat with her in the dimly lit area of the room. She held a glass to her lips as one of the men asked her a question.

"If you say it's time for the Ax, I'll go to Cosmos right now and get him. I'm surprised he ain't come on his own. He must be gone somewhere. He don't know Voo Swar's dead."

Macadoo nodded. "I'm sho' you're right 'bout that. When he knows, he'll be here. He loved that crazy voodoo woman like she was his real mama. Folks say Voo Swar took him in when his real mama died and she found out he had the mark on him. Voo Swar said his daddy was the devil himself and that's why he's the Ax. I think it's just a birthmark myself, but it sho' do look like an ax to me. It's gonna take a child of the devil to face that woman." The second man had been listening and when Macadoo finished he had his thought to share.

"I ain't never seen a black man with dogs like that before."

Macadoo understood. "And you won't see another one like him, either. There's only one black man with them devil dogs and that's the Ax."

The young man, who was sitting at the bar, stepped up to the table.

"They're called Rottweilers, Miss Macadoo, and even though they are known for their vicious nature, they are not dogs of the devil. They're just strong beautiful dogs from Italy and Germany. History tells us they were once bred to fight lions in the Roman amphitheaters. They are very loyal companions and protect their masters. They can be trained to attack and kill. They are police dogs in many countries. They haven't quite caught on here in our country, but I'm sure they will. They fight like the devil, but they are not of the devil. Miss Macadoo, you need to stop all this devil talk. Voo Swar's gone. The devil talk should be gone too. And his name is Johnny D.; Johnny D. Bryant. And, yes, he does have that ax-like birthmark on his neck, but he's not the son of the devil. He just thinks he is and he's made himself mean enough to make everybody believe it, including himself. Johnny D. Bryant is just a man from Cosmos who was raised by a crazy woman who loved scarin' the hell out of folks. They have both carried this devil thing too far. I knew him before he was the Ax. It is true, he's a bad man, but he's just a man."

Macadoo had listened to enough of the young man's philosophy. "You don't believe, do ya child?"

"I do believe in things, Miss Macadoo. I just don't believe that white woman's protected by the devil. I do believe she needs to be punished for her crimes. I hope she is, but she's just a woman. No more, no less."

Macadoo was intrigued by the handsome young man. "Ah, but this woman's more, much more. She has protectors, like the devil. Why is that?"

"I don't know if that's true. I would have to see them to believe that."

Macadoo smiled again. "Oh, I understand. You have to see things in order for you to believe they are real."

The young man smiled, too. "I have beliefs. I'm sorry I entered your conversation without your invitation." He turned away from the table.

"You don't believe in the oak tree and the oak baby?"

"No ma'am, not at all. I believe my good friends got killed because they did Voo Swar's bidding to take the child. Devil or not, if you do bring in Johnny D., please let me know when he's gonna face that white woman. I do want to be close by to see it happen." He nodded to Macadoo and went to sit at the bar with a young black woman. Macadoo looked at her two companions.

"Who is that boy?"

The older man had the answer. "That's Lamar Harris, Hattie's son. He's been gone somewhere gettin' some schoolin'. He got some money to go off to school and now he talks like that. He has a lot to say to folks."

Macadoo smiled. "I remember somethin' bout Hattie's boy bein' real smart and some men came and took him off to school. I ain't thought much more about it 'til now. He's a good lookin' thing, ain't he? And smart, too. He don't look or talk much like a Mayport boy. We need more of our young men to look and talk like that. How is Hattie anyway?"

"Not too good, I hear. She's still bad sick. That's why Lamar came home. They're expectin' the worst."

"I hate hearin' that. I like Hattie."

"We all like Hattie." Macadoo looked toward Lamar, sitting at the bar across the room.

"He don't believe, but he wants to watch that white woman fall. He's more of a believer then he knows." She smiled and touched the hand of the older man sitting to her right. "Banjo, go to Cosmos and find the Ax. Tell him what happened."

The man stood up. "Yes, ma'am."

*   *   *

The bell on the door of Miss Margaret's store sounded when Margie pushed it open. Sofia turned from her work to see her oldest sister, and relief, walk into the store. Sofia's eyes widened.

"Oh my God! You are on time to relieve me! Are you all right?"

Margie didn't smile at Sofia's unusual sarcasm.

"Don't be ugly, little sister. It doesn't look good on you." Before Sofia could respond the bell on the door rang again. The two sisters turned to see Jason and Hawk walk into the front door of the store. Margie and Sofia were both openly excited to see Jason. Hawk shook his head when he saw the amorous expressions on the two girl's faces. For a change and out of character, Sofia was the quicker of the two.

"Jason, two times in a few hours, may I help you with something?" Hawk answered.

"He needs somethin' so he don't get seasick. He used up the other pills." Margie stepped to one of the shelves and took a small box off the top shelf.

"This should do the trick." She handed it to Jason.

"Thank you."

Margie smiled as Jason walked to the counter where Sofia was standing. Hawk picked up a few items and placed them on the counter and handed Sofia money for Jason's pills and the other things. The bell on the door rang again and Mary C. walked into the store carrying Billy in her arms. She looked at the other four looking at her.

"Well, I'll be damned. It's a family reunion. I thought you'd be goin' through those jetty rocks by now and here y'all are shoppin' with my two girls."

Hawk shook his head and held up his bag of items.

"Just makin' sure Jason doesn't get sick and feed the fish all night." The bell rang on the door again. They all turned to see the Croom twins, Chuck and Buck, walk into the store. Chuck was holding a small shoebox under his arm and Buck held a cigar box with both his hands. Sofia greeted the two notoriously bad siblings.

"Hey, boys, may I help you with something today?" Chuck stood near the door, as Buck walked to Sofia and put the cigar box up on the top of the counter in front of her. There was nothing bashful about Chuck or Buck.

"We're sellin' these. Would ya like to buy one?"

Sofia smiled and opened the top of the cigar box. She screamed and pushed the box off the counter. It fell to the floor.

Everybody turned to Sofia when they heard her scream and saw the box hit the floor, spilling its contents. All the spectators watched in amazement as a number of live creatures ran all over the floor. Margie screamed, too when one of the creatures ran over her shoe. Chuck left his place at the door as two of the creatures ran toward him. As he reached down to grab the moving creatures he dropped the shoebox he was holding. When it hit the floor the top came off and more live running creatures joined the others. Mary C. moved to one side of the room with Billy. Chuck and Buck were on their hands and knees trying to recapture the wild creatures. Sofia and Margie screamed every time one of the unwelcome mystery guests would run toward them. Jason's head was on a swivel from Sofia to Margie depending on which one was screaming the loudest. Hawk shook his head and smiled.

Mary C. looked down to see one of the creatures stop next to her foot.

"Oh my God, would ya look at that. It's a real horny toad!" Sofia screamed as another horned creature ran in her direction. Mary C. was smiling. "I ain't seen a horny toad in years."

Sofia screamed. "What are they?" Mary C. kicked the one near her foot and it slid across the floor. Buck scooped the sliding critter up off the floor, as it was moving upside down past him. Mary C. knew what had invaded the store.

"Horny toads. They're horny toads. You know, them ugly lizards with horns." Margie screamed and jumped up on a chair. Chuck and Buck were rounding up the herd of horned lizards that had gotten free for the moment. The twins were laughing as they grabbed the little creatures and put them back into the boxes. It was a wild moment for Miss Margaret's store.

* * *

The black man called Banjo drove his old rusty 1953 Chevy off the ferry onto the Fort George side of the St. Johns River. He turned the Chevy left on Heckscher Drive in the direction of New Berlin. His mission was to find the Ax and tell him Miss Macadoo needed his assistance. He would be in Cosmos in twenty minutes.

* * *

The Punjabi priest stood on the dock looking down at the shrimp boat Mary C. He looked at the winch where his long hair had been entangled. He saw no evidence his hair had ever been there. The connecting wheels of the machine were clean. He relived the moment when he would have used the holy Kirpan sword to gain his freedom. He also thought of his defeat at the hands of Hawk and the circus people and he was once again ashamed. A voice brought him back to the reality of the dock.

"Somethin' I can do for you, mister?" Sandeep did not turn around. He recognized Mr. Leek's voice. "Why you here, mister?" Sandeep continued looking at the winch.

"I mean no harm to anyone, sir. I know you don't like me being here and I am very sorry for that. I will leave now." Sandeep was right about Mr. Leek's feelings about him. Mr. Leek wanted to say more to the unwelcome stranger, but he didn't want to anger the Punjabi warrior. He said nothing as the priest left the fish house and drove away in his white Mercedes. As the car pulled out onto the main road, a police car followed. Officers David Boos and Paul Short were still trailing their Punjabi priest. Once again the priest knew they were behind him, but he did not care.

*   *   *

All but one of the horned toad lizards was back in the two boxes. Hawk held up the last one to be captured. He held the strange reptile by its horns with his thumb and index finger. The strange-looking animal hung there as if it was allowing Sofia and Margie to get a better look. Mary C. had to share her thoughts.

"Ain't nothin' uglier then a damn horny toad." Hawk moved the small round-bellied lizard closer to Sofia and Margie. They both made faces and moved their heads back away from the dangling spread-eagle reptile. For some strange reason, the usually quiet Lester "Hawk" Hawkins took the attention and the floor.

"Even though the only reference you have is that they are horny toads," he looked at Mary C., "they are actually horned lizards and not toads at all. And they might just very well be the ugliest of all the lizards."

Mary C. had to speak up. "Everybody calls 'em horny toads. Nobody calls the little devils horned lizards except Mr. Lizard Man here." They all smiled at Mary C.'s remark about Hawk. Hawk smiled, too. He took the lizard and turned it on its back in his big hand. Sofia and Margie moved closer and watched with their beautiful eyes wide open. Hawk began to rub the exposed belly of the little lizard with one finger. The creature did not move. Sofia made her observation.

"Look Margie, it's asleep." Margie stepped closer.

"Oh my God, it is!" Hawk smiled. Mary C. shook her jealous head as the two girls stood close to her man and they reached out and touched the lizard's stomach. Mary C. couldn't help herself.

"If y'all reach over there and rub Hawk's belly, he'll do the same thing. He'll be snorin' in just a few seconds. I have to do that all the time." Hawk didn't respond. Sofia was excited.

"They look prehistoric, like baby dinosaurs. Like they're from another time."

Margie had her opinion, too. "They look like little devils to me." Margie looked at the twins. "Where did you find them?"

Chuck had the answer. "They'll all over the sand dunes."

Buck joined in. "Millions."

All eyes turned to Hawk when he once again, and out of character, took over the conversation. Mary C. couldn't believe her quiet and reserved man was making himself the center of attention.

"Mary C.'s right about most folks callin' 'em horny toads. It sounds better than horned lizards; more colorful. They eat ants. When I was a boy we lived in Texas for a while. They were all over the place. We used to race 'em. We even tied a

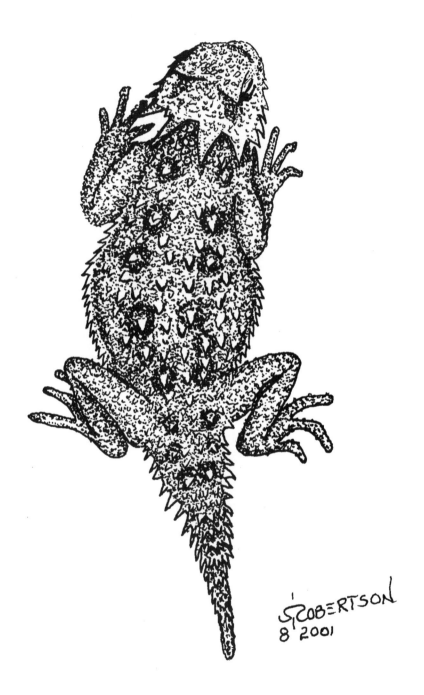

Horned Toad

string around their necks and walked 'em around like they were pets on a leash." The sisters smiled, the twins listened for a change, Jason looked at his mother and Mary C. rolled her eyes.

"The Mexicans consider them symbols of strength and they are respected for healing powers. They call them, 'Torito de la virgen'."

Sofia was enthralled. "What does that mean?"

"The virgins' little bull." Mary C.'s eyes really rolled that time. Hawk continued his surprising horny toad lesson.

"They say the toads weep tears of blood and some people hold them up as sacred creatures. Some of them have been known to squirt a red blood like fluid from their eyes when they are angry or they are in danger." The two sisters made faces again and the twins smiled at the thought of blood shooting out of the toad's eyes. "Not all of them do that. Most of the time they are very docile and easy to handle, like this one." Buck took one out of his box and held it up. He looked deep into the creatures eyes hoping for the squirt of blood that did not come. Hawk had more for his audience.

"The story goes that a group of shrimpers came back from Brownsville, Texas after the shrimp season ended there and brought back a bunch of horned toads to show their children and friends. Some were finally released into the woods and on the beaches and they have been breeding and running wild ever since. Then, another group of shrimpers brought in a batch of the little critters from Aransas Pass, Texas. They started breedin', too, and we had horned toads all over the place."

Mary C. could not allow Hawk all the attention he was acquiring.

"That ain't the only thing breedin' and runnin' wild around here." She looked at the two sisters. "Girls, y'all do know why he knows so much about horny toads, don't ya?" Mary C. did-n't care if they answered. She had her own answer to give. "It's because he's a little horny toad himself. It takes one to know one. In fact, as I look around the room, I realize there's a bunch of little horny toads in Mayport and they ain't all four-legged or in them boxes. There's a few three-legged roamin' around." Hawk looked at Mary C. and put the horned toad he was hold-ing into Buck's box. He knew Mary C. had taken her sarcasm to the final level. He looked at Jason.

"We need to get to work."

Sofia smiled at Hawk. "Thank you for telling us about the horny toads. It was very interesting." Hawk nodded and smiled, too.

"You're welcome. I hadn't thought about them in years." He walked past Mary C. near the door. She wouldn't let up on her man.

"Thank you for telling us about the Mexican virgins, too, Mr. Horny Toad." The bell on the door rang when Hawk pushed the door open. Jason followed him. Chuck and Buck followed Jason. Mary C. stepped to the counter.

"I need some powder for this baby."

Sofia screamed once more as a renegade horny toad jumped from the shelf behind her.

*   *   *

Banjo walked up to the front door of a small A-framed house. It was the same house where Jessie had taken Jason to meet her best friend, Ruby, before they embarked on their adventure to Ruskin, Florida in search of the peanut man, Tom Green. It was the same house where Ruby and Jessie danced for Jason after dinner. It was the same house where Jessie shared Jason's sexual talents with her sister-like friend, Ruby. Banjo knocked on the front door and he felt the house vibrate with heavy footsteps coming toward the door. A beautiful face peered through the small window of the door.

"Who's there?"

"It's Banjo, Miss Ruby. Miss Macadoo sent me here to see the Ax." The door opened and Ruby stepped into the light.

"It is you, Banjo. Come on in."

Banjo tried not to look at Ruby's female attributes, but she was always showing her favors, especially her huge breasts. She wore a long white nightgown. The material of the gown was thin and the light showed through it, revealing Ruby's naked body underneath. He tried not to look at her long and deep breast cleavage line, but it was near impossible not to look. He tried not to look at her bare skin when it touched and pushed against the thin cloth of the gown, but that was impossible, too. She was an incredible specimen and a true pleasure for the male eye. Her straight white teeth added to her beauty, but Banjo hadn't even considered her teeth yet. Banjo needed to say something to clear his head so he repeated his mission.

"Miss Macadoo sent me to talk to the Ax. Is he here?" Ruby knew she was the reason Banjo had lost his train of thought. She liked doing that to men and had a great deal of practice at it.

"He's here. He just got back from who knows where. He's out back with his dogs. He'd rather be with them damn dogs than with me. Would you rather be with a dog than me, Banjo?" She pushed her two major assets toward the nervous black man. He tried not to look, but he did. "Well, would ya?"

"No. Not ever ma'am."

Ruby smiled. "Come on, I'll show you where."

Banjo followed Ruby down the hall to the door that

Abaddon

opened onto the back porch. He watched her butt move under the thin gown as she walked down the hall. He had seen more of Ruby than he ever expected. The greeting at the door and the walk down the hall was worth the trip already. Banjo had no idea he would see even more of Ruby at another time. Ruby pushed the back screen door open and stepped out onto the back porch.

"Banjo's here to see you, Johnny. Don't sic the dogs on him."

Banjo stepped through the opened door and out onto the porch. Ruby rubbed against him as she moved back into the house. He tried not to react to the contact as he looked to his right to see the Ax sitting in a fan-backed wicker chair like a king on his throne. Six huge Rottweilers were sitting or lying on the floor of the porch at his feet. The dogs were all similar in size and markings, except one. They all weighed about a hundred and ten pounds, except one. The dogs looked up at Banjo, but made no noise or movement toward him, except one.

The monster Rottweiler stood up and walked slowly to where Banjo was standing near the door. Banjo was scared but he didn't move as the huge dog came closer to him. The dog stood next to the frightened black man. The animal was at least thirty pounds heavier than the other five dogs. His head looked like it was two sizes too big for its body. It was a mutant of a dog and Banjo was becoming more afraid each second he stood there. Banjo looked at the man called the Ax.

Johnny D. Bryant was his given name. His mother died during his birth and there was no record of a father. He was born with a birthmark on his neck that resembled an ax. The voodoo woman, Voo Swar, took him to raise as her own when she saw the mark on his neck. His skin was blue black. Not even Tom Green was as black as Johnny D. He was tall and powerfully built. He had high cheekbones and the look of a warrior. There was no doubt that Mandingo blood flowed in his veins.

Banjo remained standing near the door and the dog. He didn't want to move until the Ax acknowledged him. He didn't know what to do. He had never faced the Ax and did not know what to expect. Banjo looked down at the dog in front of him. All the man wanted to do was deliver the message and get away from the devil's porch. He took a chance and spoke first.

"Miss Macadoo sent me to find you. She needs you to come see her in Mayport. She wants me to tell you why, if that's all right?" Banjo's mouth was dry after he delivered the message. Johnny D. Bryant's voice was deep and raspy, like there was something wrong with his throat. Banjo was afraid when the Ax spoke to him.

"Something has happened, if Macadoo has sent you. Why didn't my mother send you?" Banjo's heart went crazy in his chest. He realized the Ax did not know the woman he called mother was dead. "I asked you a question. You have chosen not to answer it. Why is that?"

Banjo looked down at the dog. "I'm afraid."

"I ain't gonna feed the messenger to Abaddon. At least not until you tell me what I should know? I'm sure he would love to eat you, but not yet." Banjo took a deep breath. The Ax liked talking about his most vicious and favorite dog, Abaddon. "He is the true destroyer. We have the same nature, me and the dog. He kills with no feeling like it should be. He is my brother."

The Ax had given diabolical names to his six canine protectors. They were all followers and protectors of the devil. Abaddon is the devil's destroyer. Habbalah is the creature that invokes the blood lust. Calabim is the destroyer who can control his animal instincts as a member of society until the evil is needed. Shedim possesses wild animals and uses them for evil bidding. Djinn is the servant of Beelzebub who takes the form of an animal to hunt and track down the devil's victims. Lilin is the servant who brings the animal instincts out of the other servants. Johnny D. Bryant had taken his obsession with the Prince of Darkness to a strange and interesting level when it came to naming his dogs. Banjo's mouth was its driest as the devil man continued. "You ain't answered my question yet."

Banjo knew he was disturbing his host and he found the courage or perhaps the stupidity in the midst of pure fear.

"Your mother, Voo Swar, is dead. She was killed by the white woman they call Mary C. Four of Voo Swar's followers are dead, too. Also at the white woman's hand. Macadoo wants you to avenge your mother and rid the world of this woman and those who stand by her and protect her." Banjo's heart pounded in his chest when he heard the raspy voice again.

"Leave me." The Ax didn't have to tell Banjo a second time. He was through the back door, down the hall and out the front door. He didn't even consider a last look at the voluptuous Miss Ruby.

Ruby stepped to her front door as Banjo drove his Chevy away from the house. She turned when she saw a large shadow on the wall in front of her. The Ax was standing behind her. She turned to face him.

"What is it? What did Banjo want?" The Ax stepped closer and looked down on her.

"What he wanted does not concern you. What I want does." He turned and walked to a bedroom. Ruby followed him without a word. The Rottweilers would bark and howl until Ruby had satisfied the man who thought he was the devil's son. The dogs always seemed to know when Ruby was performing for their master.

CHAPTER FIVE

It was Sunday morning. Jason and Hawk were on the Mary C. about ten miles off the beach near Fernandina. They were on the stern of the boat, sitting on wooden Coca-Cola crates, picking out the shrimp and fish from the last drag as the automatic pilot guided the boat toward the jetty rocks at the mouth of the St. Johns River. The night of shrimping had not been the best they had seen, but by the look of the last drag the night would not be a total loss. There seemed to be many more fish in the catch than shrimp. Mr. Leek would buy the fish, but they would make much more money if they had the shrimp to sell. They would bring in two hundred pounds of shrimp and a thousand pounds of assorted fish, mostly Spanish mackerel. They were both tired and ready to get home to rest. The seasick pill Jason had taken had done the trick and he had only been a little nauseated through the night.

A number of sea birds had emerged from above to encircle the Mary C. The fish on the deck of the boat and the scrap fish being pushed back overboard had created a huge smorgasbord of dead fish for hundreds of hungry birds. The squawking of the seagulls as they fought over the food was annoying enough, and not Jason's favorite time as a shrimper. The worst problem with the birds was when the huge pelicans moved in and began what seemed to be an actual, intentional bombing raid on the boat and its two-man crew below. Every shrimper hated to hear that "splat" sound as the prehistoric looking birds began to empty their bellies and relieve themselves as they flew overhead. Few things stink as bad as the rotten fish smell of pelican guano.

Jason and Hawk were picking out and separating the many sea creatures that had fallen out of the net onto the deck of the boat when the first big splat hit the deck near them. They both knew it was time to take cover until the assault from the sky ended. It sounded like a muted hail storm hitting the roof and deck as Jason and Hawk watched from the safety of the wheelhouse until they thought it was safe to continue the work at hand. The birds had emptied their bellies and would fill them again as the two shrimpers worked to clean and clear the deck.

*   *   *

Mary C. started her Ford Falcon and let the engine warm up while she fixed a blanket and made Billy comfortable on the front seat next to her. Officer Jimmy Johnston stood on the front steps of the Oak Harbor Baptist Church. Al and Eloise Leek walked out of the church with their two children, Denise and Mark. Al Leek liked Jimmy Johnston. He always treated Jimmy's position as a lawman with respect.

"Mornin', Officer Johnston. I won't ask you how the law business has been this week because I know y'all have had your hands full lately."

Jimmy nodded his head. "Yes sir, there's always somethin' crazy goin' on, especially in the immediate vicinity."

Al Leek could usually get Jimmy talking. "Any more big news you can share with the public?"

"Well, you know most of the serious stuff about Mary C. and the battle royal at her place. You know about the wolf girl. Somethin' happened to that big Indian fella who was stayin' at the King house." Eloise and the children moved past the two men. Mr. Leek was interested.

"He's a strange bird, that one. I don't like him bein' around here at all. What happened to him?"

"Mr. Butler wanted to talk to him about his whereabouts the night Mary C. killed Voo Swar and those other poor devils. He thinks the Indian was there and helped her."

Mr. Leek's eyes lit up. "I didn't know that was a possibility. Pretty interesting, don't ya think?"

"Well, you have to admit it's hard to believe Mary C. did all that damage and killin' alone and he is some kind'a soldier."

Mr. Leek was as ready to listen as his information source, Officer Jimmy Johnston, was ready to share what he knew. "Well, like I said, Mr. Butler wanted me to pick the Indian up for questionin'. As soon as I got into my car to drive to the King house, a call came over the radio about a white Mercedes Benz with an injured man in it, parked in front of Tony's Seafood Shack out on Mayport Road. I knew it was the Indian."

Mr. Leek looked puzzled. "He was hurt?"

"Yeah, he was hurt, all right. His jaw was broken. He didn't say much at the time. He said he fell at the dock, but we didn't think that was true at all."

"Why didn't y'all believe him?"

"There was somethin' else wrong with him." Mr. Leek was all ears as Jimmy continued. "His hair was cut. Or I should say, it was all chopped off on one side of his head and in the back. The other side of his head still had hair eight feet long hangin' down. There was no doubt someone had done that to him when they broke his jaw. It looked like somebody took a knife and chopped it off. We found a strand of hair that was black and eight feet long on one of the men killed out at Mary C.'s."

"The hair y'all found makes Butler's idea a little more interesting, don't it?"

Jimmy wanted to change the subject. "I'm glad to have the day off. I'm gonna try and relax and not think about any of that stuff today. I didn't mean to start talkin' like that here on a beautiful Sunday mornin'." Mr. Leek wanted to hear more but he let it go. He knew he would get more from Jimmy later. He had an offer for Jimmy.

"I'll be fishin' at the little jetties with a bag full of Eloise's roast beef sandwiches and a couple of pieces of her sour cream pound cake. Should I tell her to add sweet tea for us both?" Jimmy smiled at the kind invitation and question. He did like to fish with Mr. Leek.

"Sorry Al. It sounds great, but I am committed to another engagement. And when I tell you what it is, you just might have me committed."

"It must be important for you to pass up that sour cream pound cake and fishin'." Jimmy looked over at the battle ship gray bus parked near the side of the church. The church had purchased the old used bus from the Mayport Naval Base and used it to transport children and senior citizens to the church who didn't have rides. The bus was half the size of a regular school bus. On one side of the bus was written: "Oak Harbor Baptist Church" and on the back of the bus it read: "Follow us. We're going to God's house."

"I'm takin' some of my scouts in the church bus to St. Augustine for the afternoon. We're goin' to the Gator Farm and maybe to the old fort if we have time."

Mr. Leek smiled. He did like Officer Jimmy Johnston.

"You're always doin' somethin' for those boys, ain't ya? Why in the world would you want to do that? I sure hope they appreciate all you do for them."

"They do in their own way. Some of 'em just don't know how to express their feelin's. They're getting' better at it, though."

Mr. Leek put his hand on Jimmy's shoulder. "I'll be thinkin' 'bout ya when I'm pullin' in that first big red, but I do realize you have been called to a higher purpose this fine Sunday." They both laughed as one of Jimmy's boys walked up. It was Sebastian. Jimmy turned to greet his quiet, overweight little friend.

"Well, here's one of the boys, now." Sebastian nodded. Mr. Leek took the lead.

"Mornin' son. I hear you're headed to see some gators?" Mr. Leek stuck his hand out for Sebastian to shake hands with him. Sebastian took Mr. Leek's hand, but didn't verbally respond. The trip to St. Augustine would be the first time in a year that Sebastian did anything with Jimmy and the other boys, since they found the skeletal remains of James Thorn in the woods near the Indian burial grounds out in East Mayport; a full year before. Jimmy was hoping the outing would bring Sebastian back to the group. The young boy moved away from the adults so he wouldn't have to talk. Mr. Leek looked at Jimmy.

"He's a strange little fella, ain't he?"

"Strange ain't the word for Sebastian. He's much more than strange, but he'll make it." Jimmy turned when he heard familiar voices. It was Chuck and Buck, the Croom twins. Chuck had Buck in a headlock. Or perhaps Buck had Chuck. Jimmy watched the two boys fall to the ground locked together like the Siamese twins Ming and Ling.

"Now, those two right there are even stranger than Sebastian, if you can believe it."

"You don't have to tell me about those two. They are not allowed on the dock. They are true disasters waiting to happen. Now, those two scare me. There's somethin' wrong with 'em both. They ain't right in the head." The twins got off the ground and ran past Jimmy and Mr. Leek. One of the boys slapped Jimmy on his butt as he ran by. Mr. Leek had a question.

"You ain't gonna take those two today, are ya?" Jimmy looked at Mr. Leek, but didn't answer. His eyes answered the question for him. Mr. Leek couldn't believe it. "Have you lost your mind? Those two little devils on that bus all the way to St. Augustine and then you have to keep an eye on them at the Gator Farm? You are a much better man than me, Officer Jimmy Johnston. This police work you do has taken away your reasoning ability."

Jimmy smiled. "You wanna bring Mark and Denise and go with us? I think Margie and Sofia are goin' to help with the boys. Y'all are sure welcome to come with us."

It was Mr. Leek's turn to smile. "I ain't been to that Gator Farm in years. I don't think the children have ever been. I know Eloise could use a day without them. Maybe I have a higher purpose today myself."

Jimmy couldn't believe his friend was actually considering a trip to the Gator Farm.

"We're leavin' in about half an hour and we'll be back before dark."

Mr. Leek looked at the bus and had another question. "You can drive that old bus?"

Jimmy pressed his lips together and nodded proudly. "We've got one just like it at the station. I drive it into

Jacksonville when we have to transport the prisoners to the Pea Farm. Yes sir, I can drive it."

*   *   *

Mary C. drove her Ford Falcon away from Miss Margaret's house. Sofia, Margie and Peggy were in the car with her. Sister Susan was minding the store. Miss Margaret waved good-bye to them all from the front door where she stood holding Billy in her arms. They were headed to the Oak Harbor Baptist Church. Officer Jimmy Johnston had no idea of the amount of help he was going to have on his Boy Scout trip to St. Augustine.

Jimmy Johnston, police officer, scoutmaster and chauffer sat at the wheel of the battle ship gray Oak Harbor Baptist Church fellowship bus waiting for his passengers to arrive. He still couldn't believe his friend, Al Leek, had decided to make the trip to St. Augustine and give up his Sunday fishing off the little jetties. Chuck and Buck were the first to arrive. They were side-by-side as they walked up the three steps into the bus. Jimmy greeted the troublesome duo.

"Hey fellas. Glad you could make it." The two bad boys moved past Jimmy at the driver's seat without a word and hurried to the last seat at the back of the bus. Officer Jimmy Johnston was much smarter than that.

"Before you two get too comfortable back there, your seats for the trip are right up here behind me." The twins looked at each other and frowned. "That's the deal. There will be no discussion and no negotiations, whatsoever. Take it or leave it."

Chuck and Buck knew Jimmy meant what he said. They had challenged him before and lost. The trip was too important to them to challenge him in any way. They reluctantly walked to the front of the bus and plopped their bodies into the seat directly behind the driver's seat.

"Thank you gentleman, for your cooperation." Buck stuck his tongue out, but Jimmy didn't see it. He was turning to the door of the bus because he heard footsteps. Jimmy smiled when he saw Pee Wee Croom, the twins' older, but smaller, brother boarding the bus.

"Hey Pee Wee! I was hopin' you'd be comin' with us today. It's nice to have the older brother around. Without your big brother, Joe, to keep these guys in line, you'll have to help me, if I need it." Jimmy motioned to the twins behind him. Pee Wee liked the praise he was receiving from the scoutmaster, but he knew he never did too much to help with the twins behavior. He had been double-teamed by them before. They were both bigger than him even though he was the oldest of the three. Their older brother, Joe, was not going on the trip. He was getting too old to spend much time with Jimmy and the boys. Pee Wee was usually very quiet. With two aggressive brothers like Chuck and Buck, it was easy to stay quiet. Jimmy's greeting gave Pee Wee a moment of courage. Jimmy knew what to say to make each boy feel good about himself.

"I'm glad you asked me to go. Thank you." Jimmy's heart raced in his chest when Pee Wee thanked him. The young boy climbed up into the bus and sat a few seats behind his two brothers. Mr. Leek and his two children, Mark and Denise, were the next passengers to arrive and climb into the bus. Jimmy had to speak his mind.

"I'm sorry, Al. I still can't believe you gave up a day of fishin' to go with us."

Mr. Leek smiled as he climbed up the three steps. "I just thought I'd do somethin' different on this glorious Sunday. Perhaps this is the day I can make a difference for someone."

Jimmy nodded. "That's a fact my friend." Mr. Leek and his children moved to find a seat. Chuck or Buck leaned forward and whispered to Jimmy.

"That girl ain't no scout. What's she doin' here?"

Jimmy whispered back. "She's a girl scout." Jimmy looked out the front window of the bus as the blue Ford Falcon drove into the churchyard. He couldn't believe his eyes when Mary C. and the three sisters stepped out of the car. He couldn't pass up an opportunity to tease the twins.

"Boys, here comes the rest of the girl scouts now." Chuck and Buck looked out the window to see the four women walking toward the bus. The twins looked at each other in disgust. The four women boarded the bus.

"Welcome aboard the Gator Farm Express, ladies. Watch your step and please find a seat." Jimmy spoke to each one of the women as they passed him and found a seat.

"Miss Mary C., thank you for joining us. Margie, glad to have you with us. Sofia, you are always willing to help. Thank you. Peggy, what a surprise."

"I came to see you act silly." Jimmy reached for the handle to close the door of the bus. He stopped when he saw his little friend, Sebastian, standing on the ground outside the door of the bus. Jimmy smiled.

"Hey, little buddy. You goin' with us?" Sebastian nodded and climbed the three steps. He looked at the twins briefly, but looked away and moved to a seat away from his two nemeses. Jimmy Johnston closed the door and started the engine of the bus. He looked into the rearview mirror above him and smiled at the bus full of his friends who had decided to join him on a Sunday morning. They were on an adventure outing to the Gator Farm in St. Augustine, Florida.

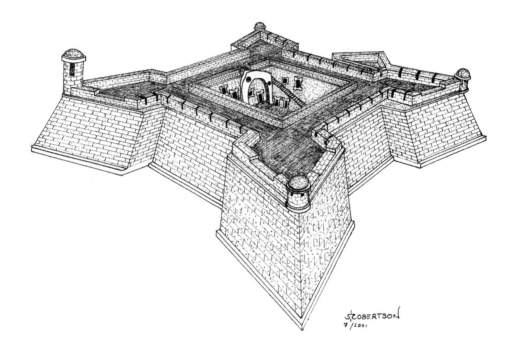

Castillo de San Marcos
St. Augustine, Florida

* * *

Hawk steered the Mary C. up next to Mr. Leek's dock. Jason jumped off the boat and onto the dock. He had a rope in his hand and he tied it to one of the dock pylons to secure the bow of the boat to the dock. Hawk came out of the wheelhouse and tossed the stern rope to Jason so he could secure it too. Jason tied the rope off and used the rubber tires that served as bumpers for the boat to rest against the dock. Hawk killed the engine.

Two of Mr. Leek's dockworkers came out of the fish house and joined Jason on the dock. They would help them unload the fish and few shrimp they had caught. Mr. Leek always took Sunday off, but he would have someone there in case a boat would have to unload.

* * *

Sandeep Singh's white Mercedes Benz was parked in front of one of the rooms at the Bennett's Motel in Atlantic Beach. The police car that had been trailing him was gone. The Punjabi priest's new bald head rested on a pillow as he slept the Sunday morning away. He was injured and needed to rest.

* * *

Jimmy Johnston's eyes were the only eyes not looking out the side window of the bus as they passed the old Spanish fort in St. Augustine. Jimmy was watching the road in front of him. He knew he was responsible for a dozen people including himself. He took his responsibility seriously, like he did most things. He knew they were only fifteen minutes away from the Gator Farm once they crossed the Bridge of Lions to the Anastasia side of the Matanzas River. He had to take the opportunity to give the boys and anyone else who wanted to listen, a history lesson.

"That's the Spanish fort, Castillo de San Marcos. The Spanish built it in the late sixteen hundreds. It's built from coquina shell stones. The same stuff we have in the coquina pits in Wonderwood near East Mayport. Coquina means 'little shells' in Spanish." The passengers were all quiet as Jimmy Johnston went on with his impressive and informative history lecture. "The famous Englishman, Sir Francis Drake, attacked St. Augustine and burned the city. The pirate, Robert Searles, attacked and looted the city. Even the ruthless General James Oglethorpe, attacked St. Augustine. The citizens of the city would go inside the walls of the fort for safety until the attack was over. Later in its history it was a holding point for the captive hostile Indians. We'll try to stop there on the way back if we have time." The bus was still quiet. Jimmy's interesting information had intrigued his captive audience. The Croom twins were still sitting directly behind Jimmy where he had put them. Chuck spoke up.

"Let's stop at the fort now. We wanna go there first."

Buck agreed. "Yeah."

Jimmy looked into the rearview mirror over his head and smiled at the twins. "Guess what?"

The twins asked their own question in stereo. "What?"

"Y'all ain't in charge." Jimmy had to tell the group one more thing. "Later I'll tell y'all about all the ghosts here in St. Augustine. You can't have an old Spanish fort and all the fightin' that went on back then without a few ghosts comin' out of the graves around here." Jimmy had timed his ghost talk perfectly as the bus drove past an old cemetery near the center of town. All eyes were wide open, including the adults'. Jimmy smiled at Mr. Leek in his rearview mirror and Mr. Leek smiled back. The Navy-battleship-gray half-bus turned east onto the

Bridge of Lions and headed toward the Gator Farm.

*   *   *

Macadoo walked out of the New Testament Zion Church off old Girvin Road. Her friend, Banjo, stepped up behind her and whispered in her ear under her wide brim hat.

"I saw the Ax last night and told him about Voo Swar. I'm not sure if he's comin', but I told him."

Macadoo reached her hand up and touched Banjo on his cheek.

"Thank you. He'll come. It just has to be on his own time and when he chooses, but he'll come."

CHAPTER SIX

MR. JOHN KING SAT AT A TABLE IN THE BIG TOP RESTAURANT AND lounge at the Giant's Motel in Gibsonton, Florida. The beautiful belly dancer, Ana Kara, sat in the booth next to him. The giant, Big Bob, and the skeleton man, Norman Bates, sat in the booth on the other side of the table. The black fat lady, Beulla, stood next to the table with a tray of coffee cups.

"This coffee smells so good. It reminds me of bein' home in Georgia." She placed a cup in front of their guest, John King, first. "John, do ya have to leave us so soon? We sure like havin' you around." The fat lady looked at Ana Kara and raised her eyebrows. Ana looked away. John King smiled.

"I need to get back home. Those ghosts get lonely without me and they might take up residence somewhere else if they think I've left them."

Ana Kara touched his thigh with a gentle hand. "Don't blame it on those ghosts. They are just fine without you for a few days. You miss them and you know it. You are a homebody and you know that, too. You've been ready to go since the first day you arrived."

Big Bob nodded and smiled too. "John, you really love that house and that little fishing village, don't you?"

Mr. King smiled at Big Bob's question. A question that was very easy for him to answer.

"Everything I am, all my feelings and any substance I may have, comes from the people who have passed through my life in that little town. I do love it there. I wish you could have seen it before the Navy took it all away."

Ana Kara looked at Big Bob and then at Mr. King. She wanted to hear more of her new friend's hometown.

"John, you have such wonderful stories about Mayport. Tell us about those good things you remember. But no ghosts please. You always catch me off guard." Mr. King smiled. He was more than willing to tell about his younger days in Mayport, Florida, U.S.A.

"When I was a boy, there was much more to Mayport than what you have seen. They took it all away in the name of national defense. The mouth of the river at the Atlantic Ocean was a perfect location for a naval base and air field." The circus family was the best group of listeners a storyteller could have. They were genuinely interested in what Mr. King had to say. They were always respectful. Mr. King continued. "Before the Navy took over, Mayport went from the river's edge to the ocean. There was the little village you have seen, there was East Mayport between the village and the ocean, there was Ribault Bay and Seminole Beach and there was Wonderwood by the Sea."

Ana Kara's eyes lit up. "What a nice name. It sounds lovely."

Mr. King nodded and smiled. "It was beautiful. The name came from a woman who owned the land. Her name was Elizabeth Stark. Folks say she came from royalty and arrived in Mayport from New York in the early 1900's. The story goes that she came to town in a golden carriage drawn by six white horses. She later had to sell the carriage when she needed money, but she always had horses on her land. At first Mrs. Stark lived in a Spanish type mansion built on Ribault Bay. She called it 'Miramar'."

Ana had to respond again. "What lovely names for places. She was very creative, wasn't she?"

"Yes, she was. The Navy took the bay and her Miramar first. Then they wiped out East Mayport. Took it all. Tore everything down including St. Johns Catholic Church. That was a beautiful little church. It had an angel on the front. I loved that church. We used to walk from Mayport to East Mayport. The short cut was believed to be haunted. It was my first introduction to the spirit world. I was about eight years old and I was one of the few young boys who really wanted to see the ghosts there. It was one of those places where the wind always seemed to be blowing. Everyone would run when the wind started to blow. I really wanted to stay and see the ghosts, but I would run when the others did." Mr. King could see his audience was captivated with his journey to his past. Ana smiled and touched his arm again. He continued.

"Mrs. Stark was a special woman. In a time when women were in the background, she was at the front and was able to hold her own. She brought a new style to Mayport. I used to love to hear her stories. Mrs. Stark was a true world traveler. She was the best storyteller of them all, because she had done so many things and been so many places. She told stories of the bullfights in Spain and it was obvious she had actually seen what she was relating. Mrs. Stark talked of her visit to the Taj Mahal and the Egyptian pyramids. No one in Mayport had ever talked of such things or places. We were all intrigued, mesmerized and in awe of the lady's adventures. It was very unusual for a woman to be so aggressive in a man's world."

Big Bob joined in. "Do you think you got your ability to tell stories from this wonderful woman?"

Mr. King smiled as if he had never thought about that possibility.

"You know, that could very well be true, or at least part of my love for tales and stories. I know that being around her was exciting and always a pleasure. Perhaps she did spark my creative juices and gave me the ability to listen. That's part of telling good stories, being a good listener. I take in everything when folks are talkin' and don't forget a thing. Between Mrs. Stark, my relatives and the ghosts around Mayport, I just had to tell stories. That Mrs. Stark, she was somethin'." Mr. King stopped and looked at his circus family. He smiled at Norman. "I hope I'm not boring, Norman. I need to be quiet for a while, don't I?"

Norman smiled back. "You couldn't bore any of us, John. We like hearing about your life and the things that make you, you. Please go on."

John didn't need much encouragement. "Another great story about Mrs. Stark is that she took a group of young Mayport girls and organized them into a Girl Scout troop. They were called the Cherokee Rose Troop Number One. She dressed the girls in khaki skirts, wide-brimmed hats, long black ties and knee-high leggings. She supplied the horses, rifles and other equipment they needed, as well as a place to train. The girls rode the beaches during the war and patrolled the area for any enemy action along the shores. Some times they would camp out all night up in the sand dunes on the beach as part of their wartime duties, watching for any communication from the shore to enemy forces out in the ocean. They were ready to alert the citizens of an enemy invasion. It's another great Mayport story and I'll bet it was a first. Women were not put in many dangerous situations and Elizabeth Stark had young girls riding the beaches with guns, watching for the enemy to arrive by sea. It had to be a first."

Ana had to interrupt. "John, this is great history. These are wonderful stories."

Mr. King had more. "We used to love the Easter egg hunts at Miss Stark's house. There was always plenty of cakes and candy. And she gave all the children in Mayport a Christmas present from Santa every year. And later, when I was a man, she had a herd of goats. The horses were gone. I never understood that. I wish I would have asked about those goats. The Navy took Mrs. Stark's land and Wonderwood by the Sea was gone."

Ana looked sad and Big Bob was more than interested.

"John, Ana's right. What an interesting part of Florida history. I've never heard of such a thing. No telling how many wonderful stories and historical moments have gone by with no one knowing about them. Tell us more about your boyhood memories in this little village."

Mr. King loved the way his friends talked. He felt good about telling of his past. "As children we were allowed to move about with very little restrictions. We were all the same. Everybody took care of everybody. You had to learn to swim early because we were always around the water. One of the adults usually just threw one of us in the water and watched over us until we started swimming. It sounds cruel, but it usually worked. The few times it didn't work, the non-swimmer would be rescued before they went down under the water the third time."

Ana wrinkled her nose. "That's awful, John. They just threw y'all in?"

Big Bob joined in. "I've heard about children learning to

swim like that. It scares them into swimming. It's a survival thing. It took me forever to learn to swim. If someone would have thrown me in the water as a boy I would have drowned."

When Bob stopped, Mr. King knew he was to continue. "As I got older we would walk to Seminole Beach and swim in the ocean. We would catch blue crabs underneath the South jetties and climb up into the big rocks to catch many different fish. My two favorites were sheepshead and drum. They were fun to catch and good to eat."

Ana had a question. "What's a drum?"

Mr. King smiled. "It's a big ol' striped fish that likes to swim around those rocks." Mr. King had one more thought to share with his friends. "You know they call folks from Mayport, 'Minorcans', don't ya?"

Big Bob nodded his head. "I've been to Minorca, but I didn't know the people from Mayport were from there."

Ana looked at Big Bob. "Where's that?"

"It's a lovely island off the coast of Portugal. Are the Mayport citizens of Portuguese descent?"

"That's right. They say a large group came here from Minorca to escape the famine of the island and find a better life. That didn't happen at first. They were political and financial slaves in New Smyrna for a decade, found freedom and asylum in St. Augustine before many moved to Mayport to find work and land to settle. Not all the Mayport citizens have Portuguese blood, but the name Minorcan has stuck to all who live there. The Arnau, Andreu, Roland, Canova, and Floyd families are a few of the true Minorcans. Maybe one day I'll introduce y'all to the greatest storyteller of them all. Captain Leon Canova, the black Minorcan. That's just one of his many names."

Ana's eyes lit up. "Oh, John! He does seem interesting. The

Black Minorcan. He sounds like he would fit with our family quite well. Is he African?"

Mr. King smiled. "No, he just tans real dark. That Portuguese blood in his veins, I guess. His rivals called him that in anger. It wasn't his most coveted name. They even called him Turnbull after the ruthless Scotsman who held the Minorcans as slaves for ten years."

Big Bob joined in again. "I read about Turnbull here in Florida. He wanted to produce indigo, but he had his troubles. Shipwrecks, losing slaves, malaria and natural disasters did him in. They say he was a strong enterprising man in his early prosperous years, but defeat and failure made him cruel and he was even considered evil by some."

Ana Kara shook her head at Big Bob's interesting and informative words.

"Bob, is there any thing you don't know about? You are the most well-read man on this Earth." She looked at Mr. King. "You two are amazing."

Mr. King smiled. "You flatter me. But, I am not even close to the category with Bob. I know of my home. He knows of the world. His travels are so vast and he has seen so much. I only wish I had been all the places he has been. Too bad Mrs. Stark ain't still with us. They could really share some great stories."

Big Bob knew Mr. King wanted to get on the road and head in the direction of his beloved Mayport.

"John, you flatter me. I could listen to you talk about the old days all day, but I know you are being kind to our inquisitive nature and we thank you for indulging us. We would also like to thank you for all you've done for us and for Beth. No one has become a part of our family so quickly. You are a rare individual and you do fit in with us. Your kindness will never be forgotten and you are always welcome to be with us wherever we may be."

Ana Kara smiled, squeezed John's thigh, leaned forward and kissed him on his cheek. "Thank you, John. And promise you will come back and tell us more about Mayport."

Mr. King nodded and smiled. "Maybe y'all will pay me another visit and I'll add a few ghost stories to the package."

Ana had to smile, too. "I'm sure you will."

* * *

Officer Jimmy Johnston turned the steering wheel of the bus to the right. The gravel crunched under the tires as the bus rolled into the parking lot of the St. Augustine Gator Farm. He looked up into the rearview mirror above him again and scanned the crowd sitting behind him. He still couldn't believe he had a half busload of his friends. He pushed the brake pedal down as he stopped the bus in the shade of a large oak tree. The Mayport citizens had arrived.

There was only one short line at the small ticket booth. Jimmy waited in the line to get tickets for everyone. They all stood near the main entrance waiting for Jimmy. Mary C. was standing near the three sisters. She had an observation.

"I remember the one time I was here they had a donation bucket at the door. You gave what you could to go in the place."

Mr. Leek nodded in agreement. "That's right, Mary C. I remember that, too. I think I dropped a quarter in the pot the last time I was here, but that was years ago." Jimmy arrived with the tickets. He handed the adults their tickets first. The animated faces on each child showed their excitement. Chuck and Buck stepped up to the excited and unsuspecting Sebastian. They had to torment the weaker young man. It was part of their twisted nature. Chuck was first.

"Hey fat boy. You're gonna pee on ya'self when they ask you to hold one of them baby gators." Sebastian found a little courage.

"No I won't. Maybe you will."

Chuck wasn't prepared for Sebastian's verbal comeback and aggressive stand. He didn't like it at all. Buck jumped in.

"Look at his eyes. He's already scared. He might not pee. He might shit in his pants."

Jimmy Johnston stepped to the boys to give them their tickets. He looked at the foul mouthed, Buck.

"Another cuss word from anyone and they will spend the rest of the day in the bus." He handed the boys their tickets. Chuck and Buck knew Jimmy was serious and they would take no chances. The twins glared at Sebastian as they moved away from him.

The Mayport dozen gave their tickets to the ticket taker at the gate, one at a time, and moved into the main entrance that led to the doorway to the man-made wooden decks and walkways. They all moved to a deck area surrounded by Florida trees and plants. Jimmy gathered his group of travelers before they entered the area called the swamp. He knew what to expect and needed to set some guidelines and rules for the boys. Mr. Leek moved close to Jimmy with his two children at his side.

"I wonder if ol' Possum Willie's still wrestlin' gators here? He's probably too old now. That was years ago, but he could sure put on a show. He kept the crowd on its feet. He was the best." As if someone was listening to Mr. Leek, an announcement came over the loud speaker, mounted on the top of the main building.

"Hello visitors and welcome to the Gator Farm. We are about fifteen minutes away from another display of bravery beyond your wildest dreams. Please join Chief Sammy Panther, our resident Seminole Indian. He will demonstrate the true art of alligator wrestling for your entertainment and amazement."

Mr. Leek smiled. "I guess that answers my question about ol' Possum Willie."

Jimmy stopped the twins from going past him as they followed the directions of the announcement.

"Hold on there, fellas." He stopped them by holding his hand out in front of them. Jimmy still had to set the rules for a day with the gators.

"When we get on the deck and walk around the swamp you boys do not lean over the rails or sit on the rails, and for God's sake don't play around or tease each other. It is dangerous enough without y'all horse playin'." Jimmy looked at the young faces around him. "Stay together and remember the most important rule of the Gator Farm is that if you do happen to fall in the swamp, especially during the feedin' time, nobody's comin' in after you." All eyes of the Mayport eleven opened wide. Mr. Leek smiled. The three sisters, Sofia, Margie and Peggy all had open mouth syndrome. It was obvious that the boys were mentally processing what Jimmy had just said. He had more. "If you fall in near me, I will just look over the railing and ask you if there's anything you'd like me to tell your mama." Mr. Leek turned away from the others to keep from laughing. Mary C. smiled too. Peggy was the first adult to respond.

"That's awful. You're scarin' us all."

Jimmy kept his serious Gator Farm rule face. "If someone was to jump in to save you they would be lost, too, and we would lose two friends. If someone falls in near you just wave

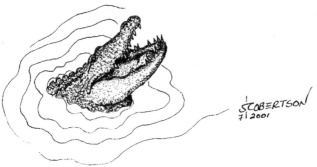

Patience

good-bye and move on to the next exhibit. If you hear a splash and then screamin' don't look, just move on."

Mary C. was getting a kick out of Jimmy's lesson. She joined in the morbid fun. "I sure ain't jumpin' in after nobody. If you're that careless you need to be ate up."

Jimmy nodded. "O.K now. Let's go have some fun and see the Seminole wrestle a gator."

The Mayport dozen walked down a long wooden deck structure. There were a few separate areas with one or two gators below. They all stopped to see what was in the exhibit. The few gators they could see were not very active. Most were lying on the ground keeping as cool as they could. Mr. Leek had a suggestion.

"Let's keep movin' to see the Seminole and then we'll stop at these places later." They moved along the decks as a group. All the Mayport eyes widened when they turned a corner and looked down at an incredible sight, wall-to-wall baby gators.

There were hundreds of the small reptiles swimming and crawling all over each other. They had to stop and watch the wild scene. Everyone was excited about what they were watching. Each baby gator was the same size as the other. No one in the Mayport group had even seen such a sight. The announcer's voice called over the loud speaker again.

"Our demonstration will begin in a few minutes. If you are interested, please move to the gator pit on the near side of the swamp." Jimmy and Mr. Leek moved the group in the direction the voice suggested. As they moved, the announcer offered more. "As you move about the farm today, please be careful of the nesting birds. You will see hundreds of newborn chicks and many eggs waiting to hatch. These Florida birds have chosen the safety of the farm because the many small animals that usually steal their eggs and raid their nests cannot get to them here in the swamp." The group stopped again when they saw the nesting birds. All eyes were glued to the hundreds of nests in the trees around them. They could reach out and touch the birds from the high decks. They were actually standing in the tops of the trees with the baby birds and the nesting adults. The entire farm had become a rookery for a number of Florida birds. The black legs and yellow feet of the snowy egrets filled hundreds of limbs. The short-legged green herons stood as tall as they could guarding the new fluffy arrivals. The birds could lay, incubate and hatch their next generation in the safety of the Gator Farm. A huge population of white ibis covered one section of trees. Newly-hatched baby birds were moving in the nests, while some eggs needed more time to crack open.

The Mayport group walked slowly as they watched the wondrous sight of the hundreds of adult birds standing guard over their young. Another interesting sight was the number of alligators floating in the water below the bushes and trees, waiting for one of the baby birds to lose its balance and fall into the water below.

The Croom twins stood together on one of the high decks next to a tree full of nesting birds. There were a number of new snowy egret hatchlings moving in the nests and chirping, waiting for their mothers to return with a tasty minnow from the water below. Chuck watched the newborn birds for a second as they fell and stumbled in the twig-filled nest. Chuck looked down and saw two alligators in the water below the deck. Then he looked up at a nest containing two moving little white feather balls. He reached out and shook one of the limbs where a nest of two baby white egret chicks was attached. His brother Buck's eyes opened wide as the two white baby birds chirped in fear as they fell out of the nest and into the water below. The two helpless birds were not in the water more than a few seconds before they were swallowed by the two alligators that had been waiting patiently below. Patience is an alligator's virtue. The two mean brothers pushed at each other and moved away from the crime scene and the evil deed they had so willingly perpetrated. Their older, but smaller brother, Pee Wee, saw the evil deed, but he would not tell on them. He didn't want to be the next one to fall in the water. The twins hurried and caught up with the rest of the Mayport group as they all walked to an open area where they moved over to stand next to a walled enclosure.

The wall was about four feet high and the spectators were finding places to stand along the concrete barrier. The Mayport twelve moved into their positions at the wall and looked down into the circular pit where a group of Florida alligators were lying like huge tree logs on the grass, on the dirt, and floating in the small water-filled pool in the middle of the enclosure. Jimmy stood at the chest high wall and looked over his group, making sure he had everyone he should have. They were all present, even the twins. The space along the wall filled quickly with spectators as they all tried to find a good spot to see the action. Sebastian looked up from his place on the wall as a man stepped up next to him and moved Sebastian to the side with his hand.

"Excuse me young man. Would you like to go with me into the gator pit?" Sebastian's face turned snow white. The twins were almost right. He was about to pee in his pants as he looked into the coal black eyes of the Seminole Indian, Chief Sammy Panther. His shoulder-length straight black hair was parted in the middle of his head. He took Sebastian's shaking hand. The young boy was scared.

"Please keep this for me in case I don't return from the pit.

There is always that sad possibility." The Indian placed a muli-colored beaded bracelet around Sebastian's wrist. Then with one athletic motion the Indian jumped over the wall and land-ed softly on his bare feet near the biggest alligator in the circle. The Indian crouched down as he landed. The crowd was excit-ed and made noises, but no yelling or clapping. They could sense the seriousness of his dangerous position. It was always exciting when there was a possibility someone could be eaten alive. It had the potential to be a real crowd pleaser. Sammy Panther put his finger to his lips and the mumblings in the crowd stopped instantly.

The Croom twins stared at Sebastian. They looked at his gift from the Seminole Indian. Jimmy smiled at Sebastian's good fortune. Chuck and Buck hated Sebastian even more than they did before, if that was possible. All eyes went back to the circle when a few women screamed and a collective gasp came from the crowd as Sammy Panther jumped from his crouching position and landed on the back of the biggest alligator in the circle. He straddled the huge scaly back with the inside of his thighs squeezing the sides of the beast. The wild Indian reached forward and grabbed the long wide snout of the gator and pulled its head backward toward him.

Sammy Panther amazed the crowd when he put his chin on the bottom of the gator's mouth, keeping the reptile's mouth closed by the pressure of the brave Indian's chin. He held his hands over his head, as he remained chin-to-chin with the water dragon of the South. The crowd exploded into cheers, whistles and clapping as Sammy released the gator and moved away to another corner of the circle. The huge gator moved away, also, and slid into the water of the pool. The loud speak-er cracked and a voice boomed over the cheering crowd.

"Ladies and gentlemen. It is an honor and privilege to present to you, a true Seminole Indian Chief, our own Sammy Panther." The crowd and the Mayport dozen clapped and cheered together. The speaker blasted again.

"What you see before you are fine adult specimens of the magnificent, dangerous and sometimes deadly, American alligator. They can run at eleven miles an hour. Although you can hold an alligator's mouth closed with minimal pressure from a few fingers, once they open their mouth they bite down with a pressure of two thousand pounds per square inch and they strike with the speed of a Florida rattlesnake. They can kill you with the sweep of their powerful tails or knock you off your feet and then eat you. They have been known to take the legs out from under big animals like horses and cows with their tails.

The largest alligator on record is over nineteen feet long. The Florida state record is a male out of Seminole County at fourteen feet. When they get that big they all weigh in the area of a thousand pounds or more. They live for about thirty years and are one of the most primitive creatures on earth today, having existed for thousands of years in the same form as they appear now. Some people call them modern day dragons and others call them the last of the dinosaurs."

Sofia turned to Margie. "We saw some little dinosaurs in the store yesterday, didn't we?"

Margie smiled. "Sofia, you are so silly."

Chuck and Buck looked at each other and smiled as they recalled the horny toad invasion at Miss Margaret's store. Mary C. had to smile, too. The voice on the loud speaker was still booming above them.

"You see them lying there as if they are asleep or too lazy to move their massive bodies, but we all know that is their trick. By the time the unwary prey gets too close, it is far too late. They'll be crushed in the jaws, pulled into the water and the gator will start to spin like a whirling dervish while holding on to the hapless victim under water. Body parts will be twisted off and devoured."

Peggy turned to Jimmy. "You left that out of your speech awhile ago. Did you forget the whirling dervish part of your description?" Jimmy smiled at Peggy's sarcasm as the voice continued.

"Our star performer, Chief Panther, has grown up in the Florida swamps and knows the alligators as a brother. He understands the creature and can do things with the gators that would get a normal man killed or seriously maimed. Although he risks serious personal harm or even death, he is going to amaze you with his ability to control these vicious creatures."

All the members of the Mayport group were quiet, interested observers. Even the twins were listening and paying attention.

Margie leaned to Jimmy and whispered in his ear. "Would you wrestle one of those things for me, big boy?"

Jimmy didn't hesitate with his answer. He whispered back to her. "I wouldn't wrestle one of those things if my mama asked me to."

The roar of the crowd ended Margie's questioning of Jimmy's love for her as Sammy approached another large gator and clapped his hands in front of its snout. When the gator leapt and snapped its jaws inches from his hand, Sammy jumped on the gator's back. The mighty gator began writhing and slashing its tail from side to side, but Sammy held on as he lay vertically on the gator's back. He had his arms and legs wrapped around the gator's body. Sammy turned the gator onto its back and began to rub its belly. The wild movement from the beast calmed as the belly rub continued. Although the loud speaker was announcing that Sammy Panther had put the great beast to sleep with a belly rub, the real reason the gator was incapacitated was because the creature, having rarely, if ever, been turned on his back, was experiencing a change in blood flow to its brain which mesmerized it. Sammy Panther stood up, lifted both hands over his head and moved away from the sleeping gator.

Sofia couldn't help it. "Look Margie, just like when Mr. Hawk rubbed the horny toad on its belly. Can you believe this?" Margie shook her head at Sofia's excitement. Peggy had to speak up.

"What are you two talking about? What in the world is a horny toad?"

Sofia leaned toward Peggy as the crowd roared again. "I'll tell you about them later."

The spectators began clapping with appreciation.

The gator didn't seem quite as dangerous as it did a few minutes before. The loud speaker boomed again.

"And now you will witness the feat that few men on this earth can do or would attempt to do." Sammy Panther walked over to another one of the big alligators and once again positioned himself on its back. This time, however, he slid both of his hands to the top and bottom jaws and held the mouth open. The gator didn't move as Sammy crawled off its back and moved in front of the gaping mouth. While holding the jaws open, Sammy Panther passed his entire head through the mouth and out the other side and then he repeated the maneuver and moved his head back though the teeth-filled jaws. When Sammy let go of the jaws and stood up straight, the jaws slammed shut like a thirty-pound bear trap. The crowd went wild and a few women screamed at the noise that was made by the jaws snapping

together. It was, no doubt, an eerie and frightening sound.
Sammy Panther moved away from all the gators and jumped up
onto the wall where he had earlier left Sebastian. In one move,
the Indian stood next to Sebastian again.

"You may keep the bracelet. Think of Sammy Panther
when you talk to your God."

The Indian was gone. The Mayport group stood there with
their mouths open. It was exciting to have the star of the show
standing with them and actually talking to Sebastian. They all
gathered around him to see the gift from the Chief. Neither
Chuck nor Buck stood near him. The voice on the speaker continued.

"And now, ladies and gentlemen, it is feeding time in the
swamp. If you will make your way to our swamp, you will be
able to witness the ferociousness of alligators when they feed.
Just follow the arrows and the signs, which will lead your way
down the path to the swamp. Thank you for your attention
during the show. Enjoy the rest of your day with us. And
remember, do not sit on or lean over the rails in the swamp. If
you were to fall in during the feeding frenzy, no one would be
able to save you." Peggy and the group looked at Jimmy after
the scary announcement. He smiled and led the way to the
swamp.

As the group moved from the round enclosure toward the
swamp they walked down a path bordered on one side by a
four-foot high fence, constructed of four-by-four posts and
heavy gauge hog wire. The sign on the fence read: "Home of
Goliath. The world's largest living alligator." Inside the fenc-
ing, basking in a water pool was a mammoth alligator, a thir-
teen footer. It was floating on the surface of the water with part
of its upper body, eyes and nose exposed. It looked as if someone had cut a limb from the giant oak tree in Mayport and

tossed it into the water. The gator's unblinking eyes seemed to be watching each individual who passed by. They all stopped for a better look at the monster. One of the farm workers stepped through the crowd and took a long cane pole, reached out and unhooked the latch on a gate at the other side of Goliath's pen. The worker pushed the gate open with the pole and the monster gator moved quickly through the opened gate and out of sight. The worker turned to the crowd that had been watching him.

"We let Goliath go into the swamp for the feeding. Folks like to see him when the frenzy is in full gear. We'll entice him back here later with more food."

They all moved to the swamp area to get a good position to watch the feeding. The Mayport dozen continued to stay together like Jimmy had requested. It was the safest way to keep track of the young people. Even the twins were following Jimmy's rules for Gator Farm safety. The voice from the loud speaker got everyone's attention once more.

"Please direct your attention to the platform on the far side of the swamp." Everyone looked at the platform as a young worker dressed like an Everglades ranger stepped out onto a platform that was only a few feet above the water level of the swamp. It was obvious to the spectators that only the biggest gators swam in the swamp. It was also obvious the gators knew it was feeding time as they jostled for the best positions near the platform. The noise from the crowd was the only introduction Goliath needed as he entered the swamp area. The announcer added to the excitement.

"Ladies and gentlemen! Goliath has entered the swamp. Do not allow small children to be on the railings." The crowd moaned in fear and many of them stepped back from the railings for a moment as Goliath swam by. Sofia took Peggy's arm.

Margie moved next to Jimmy. Sebastian did, too. Chuck and Buck did, too. Mark and Denise moved next to their father.

Mary C. never moved from her spot at the railing as the monster reptile swam past her. The announcer's voice filled the air as Goliath swam toward the feeding platform.

"Our feeder today is a brave volunteer from Jacksonville's Lee High School. Please welcome Coach Leon Barrett, football coach, educator and avid hunter." The crowd clapped for the man standing on the platform next to three garbage cans. "We usually feed the gators chickens when we can get them, but today Mr. Barrett has supplied us with all the deer meat we need to fill up these hungry gators. As a University of Georgia football alumni, I'm sure Coach Barrett would rather be feeding a bulldog than a gator, but he's a good sport today and he's going to help us feed the gators." The crowd clapped again as Coach Barrett reached into one of the cans and pulled out a huge piece of meat, dripping with blood, and threw it into the air over the water.

Like a missile launched from under the water, Goliath's huge head and half his body came up out of the water and plucked the hunk of meat out of the air before it hit the water. Everyone watching made a noise of some kind. Leon Barrett began throwing chunks of the deer meat into the water of the swamp. The gators went into a feeding, fighting frenzy as the sound of the meat hitting the water rang the dinner bell in their prehistoric heads. The gators went crazy as they battled for the bloody pieces of meat. No piece of meat stayed floating on the water for more than a second or two. The water was swirling with a feeding frenzy unmatched in the animal kingdom. At one time at least three of the gators were under one section of the observation deck fighting for the meat. The spectators had to hold on to the railings as the deck moved while the gators pushed against the pylons below. Women screamed and men held their loved ones close until the fight was over and the gators moved from under the deck and back to the center of the swamp.

Leon Barrett had emptied two of the cans and he was reaching for the last few pieces of meat in the third can. None of the workers or the spectators were prepared for the frenzy that the taste of the fresh deer meat would cause among the hungry gators. After becoming used to eating the chicken, the bloody deer meat awakened primordial behavior in the powerful primitive beasts. The scene became dangerous. The crowd roared as Goliath came out of the water and landed on the platform, shaking the entire structure. Somehow, Leon Barrett was able to keep his composure and his balance when the monster alligator hit the platform. Leon moved quickly away from the unwanted intruder and climbed up the ladder on the platform to safety.

The crowd roared and women screamed when Goliath rammed his snout into the three garbage cans, like a bowling ball knocking down extra big pins. The meat remaining in the third can fell onto the floor of the platform and the huge gator turned his head sideways and gobbled it up to the wild cheering of the ruthless blood-lusting spectators. Leon Barrett looked down from the deck above the platform as the monster slid his massive body back into the water. It would be Leon Barrett's last gator feeding unless he was feeding gator meat to a bulldog.

In spite of Goliath's gluttonous behavior, the other gators had eaten their fair share of the butchered bounty. Even though the actual feeding was over, they continued swimming in a frenzied mode, waiting for the sound of meat hitting the water. The crowd was still buzzing with the wild action they had just

The Fall

witnessed. Goliath was swimming in a speed circle from one side of the swamp to the other. His huge tail was swishing back and forth as it propelled him through the water.

Officer Jimmy Johnston moved next to Mary C. to look over the railing and watch the creature swim by the deck they stood on. The beast rounded the corner and swam directly under the wooden slats where Mary C. was standing. Jimmy turned when he saw Sebastian bend over on the deck. The young boy had dropped the beaded bracelet the Indian had given him on a wooden slat of the deck. Jimmy smiled and Sebastian smiled back as he picked up the bracelet. At that moment Goliath's massive tail hit one of the pylons as he made his pass under the deck.

Officer Jimmy Johnston was horrified when he saw Sebastian stumble, lose his balance and fall through the wooden railing and over the side into the gator infested water. No one heard him, but Jimmy said out loud, "Oh shit!" He had broken his cussing rule and wished he could go sit on the bus the rest of the day. He would have to break another of his rules when he went into the water. Real heroes have to break the rules every now and then.

With one motion, Jimmy placed both his hands on the top board of the railing and vaulted his trembling body over the railing and into the water. Margie screamed when she saw Jimmy go over the side. Only Jimmy had seen Sebastian fall. The splash that Sebastian made when he hit the water had already alerted the still hungry gators, but the second splash brought the masses.

Jimmy landed in the water right next to a panicked and terrified Sebastian, who was splashing and struggling to keep his head above the water. Women in the crowd began screaming in horror and men yelled for help when they realized what was happening. With the same fluid motion of Jimmy's jump into the water, he moved to Sebastian's side, put his hands around the boy's waist and pushed the young overweight boy up out of the water and toward the dock above. Mr. Leek and Mary C. grabbed both of Sebastian's arms and in one strong and coordinated pull, the boy was back on the deck. The crowd cheered as the three sisters moved to comfort Sebastian.

Jimmy knew the beasts were coming. He reached up to grab Mr. Leek's extended hand, but he had to look behind himself as he made the grab. It didn't matter where Goliath was located. They were all coming. He could see the bubbling and churning water behind him. Mr. Leek held Jimmy's right hand. Mary C. grabbed for his left hand like she had done to Sebastian. She missed his hand as the gators collided with Jimmy Johnston's extended body. The last eyes Jimmy Johnston would look into were Mary C.'s eyes. Mr. Butler had been right about the Mayport angel of death.

The power of the vicious contact knocked Jimmy under the deck, pulling him out of Mr. Leek's grasp. The deck shook under their feet as the gators fought for position and tore Jimmy Johnston to pieces with their powerful jaws and spinning techniques.

The spectators were running, sitting, crying and screaming, all in horror and disbelief. An eerie silence came over the swamp as the gators swam out from under the deck as if they had all taken a bite of the human who dared to enter their domain. A voice yelled, "There he is!" as Jimmy's shirt floated up onto the surface of the water. It looked as if part of his upper body and his head were still in the shirt. Mary C., Mr. Leek and the twins were the only ones from Mayport watching when Goliath's huge head slammed into what was left of Officer Jimmy Johnston. The eerie silence remained as the monster

Goliath swam away with Jimmy's shirt hanging out of the side of his mouth.

*   *   *

Lester "Hawk" Hawkins sat up in his bed. He wasn't sure why. A dream perhaps, but he didn't like the feeling he had at that moment. He laid his head back on the pillow. Sleep took his feeling away.

*   *   *

Margie and her two sisters were sitting in the main office of the Gator Farm. They were all in shock and sitting quietly. Sebastian sat on a couch with a big beach towel wrapped around his wet body. His return to scouting was short lived. He had been the victim of two life-changing experiences with Officer Jimmy Johnston. One in the deep woods at the Indian mounds and now at the Gator Farm. The sight of James Thorn's bones had haunted him for over a year and now the sight of Jimmy Johnston being eaten alive would haunt him forever.

The others of the Mayport group were sitting together on benches next to the gift shop. No one was talking. Mary C. and Mr. Leek stood with two park rangers and two St. Johns County police officers. One of the park rangers was doing the talking.

"We have not recovered any remains at all. That's not to say something won't float up later, but it's not very likely at this point." Mr. Leek nodded his head.

"I need to get these young people back home to their families. Is it all right for us to leave now?" The ranger looked at the police officer.

"I don't see why not. We can get in touch with you if we

need to later. Thank you for talking to us and we're deeply sorry about your friend and this awful tragedy. Do be careful on the way back home." Mr. Leek shook the man's hand and he and Mary C. went to gather the others. Mr. Leek went to get the young people while Mary C. went to get Sebastian and the three sisters. Mary C. passed a poster of Goliath on the wall. She knew Hawk was right and the day surrounded by the scaly-back, hard lucks had only brought misery and sorrow. She would never say the word "alligator" again. Chuck stood up from the bench he was sitting on when he saw Mr. Leek walking toward them. He had an important question for Mr. Leek.

"Who's gonna drive the bus home?"

Buck had an even more important question. "Are we still gonna go to the fort?"

CHAPTER SEVEN

THREE DAYS HAD PASSED SINCE THE GATOR FARM FEEDING FRENZY tragedy and the premature death of a true modern day hero, Officer Jimmy Johnston. The citizens of the Mayport village who knew the young police officer were shocked and saddened at the news and the circumstances of his gruesome death. The local Times-Union newspaper had given details and information about the young and respected police officer's accomplishments and very short life. Margie had been in her bedroom for the majority of three days, but she had now joined her mother and sisters to attend the funeral service for her friend and occasional sex partner. Sofia and Peggy had not said very much about the ordeal as the three days went by. Mary C., Hawk and Jason were also dressing for the funeral. They would ride together to the Oak Harbor Baptist church to pay their respects to Jimmy.

The churchyard was filling up with all types of vehicles, especially police cars. The building was full of uniformed police officers from Atlantic, Neptune and Jacksonville Beaches, as well as the City of Jacksonville and surrounding counties. The close knit fraternity of policemen came out in full force to honor and mourn the heroic legacy left behind by a fellow member of their protective society. There was no way to seat all the friends and relatives who had come to pay their respects to the popular young man. It was a standing room only crowd with at least two hundred more standing outside.

Sebastian sat with his father up front on the second row. He had been like Margie and spent the last three days in his room. Even though the weak and passive young man had witnessed the unforgettable tragedy and he would be haunted by it for years to come, his father knew Sebastian had to pay homage to the man who had sacrificed his life to save his. Sebastian looked at the pictures of Jimmy and touched the beaded Indian bracelet he still wore on his wrist. Life in Mayport had become too traumatic for the sensitive Sebastian and his family would move away from the village of shrimpers a few weeks after Jimmy Johnston's funeral.

The Croom twin's older brother, Joe, sat near the front of the church with his little brother Pee Wee. Pee Wee loved Jimmy Johnston more than any of the other boys in his Rampart 7 Boy Scout troop. The young man cried when he saw the pictures of his friend on the altar. Joe put his arm around his little brother to comfort his sorrow. Chuck and Buck were dressed for the funeral but they were not in the church. Joe had lost them in the crowd and they had stayed outside. They were hiding on the battleship gray church bus that had taken them to the Gator Farm only three days before.

Mr. Butler was standing with Paul Short and David Boos when Mary C. entered the back of the church. He stared at her when she walked down the isle of the church with Hawk and Jason at her sides. She didn't notice his stare, but she wouldn't have cared if she had seen him.

Mary C. looked at the table in front of the altar lined with pictures of Jimmy in different phases of his life. The biggest picture on display was of Jimmy in his police uniform the day he graduated from the police academy. He looked proud and handsome. Other pictures were of a freckled face little boy and a young teenager on the beach, fishing, swimming and playing football for Fletcher High School. It was a true life span pictorial of a native son.

Miss Margaret and her four daughters joined Jimmy's family members in the front two rows of pews. Every young and old policeman and every male civilian from the area watched Miss Margaret's four beautiful girls walk down the isle. Sofia's long blonde hair seemed to shine as it moved back and forth down her back, rubbing and touching her tiny waistline. She was tall and all legs. Margie's appearance was in contrast to her little sister. She had short hair and a hard body. Her sleeveless black dress revealed her tanned round shoulders and muscular arms. Not many women had her look in those days. Margie wore sunglasses to hide her bloodshot eyes.

Peggy's raven black hair was as long as Sofia's, and she usually wore it in one long braid. She had chosen to free her hair from the braids and allow it to flow off her shoulders and down her back. She had the same ice-blue eyes as Sofia, but her dark features gave her the more exotic look. Susan had blazing, dark auburn hair. She kept her usual ponytail and every man watched it brush against her lower back as she walked by. They were hypnotized as they followed that red ponytail until she sat down. Jason relived his sexual encounter with each sister. His blood boiled with lustful thoughts as he sat in the Oak Harbor Baptist Church.

With so many people in a small building, even whispers filled the room with noise. Most of the talk was about the four sisters who had taken everyone's attention as they walked by.

Mary C. leaned toward Hawk and moved her lips close to his ear.

"Did you have to look at all four of their butts as they walked by?"

Hawk shook his head at her surprising question and her jealousy. He had to respond. "I didn't want to be the only one who didn't look." The whispering and mumbling in the congregation stopped when the full-time fish house owner and part-time Baptist Deacon, Mr. Al Leek, stepped up to the pulpit to address Jimmy Johnston's family and friends. He was the perfect choice for the eulogy.

"It has been said, there is no greater sacrifice than to give up one's life to save another."

* * *

Johnny D. Bryant, the Ax, put his six Rottweiler dogs into a hunting dog box cage in the back of his black El Camino. Abaddon was the last of the dogs to jump up into the back bed of the black truck. Johnny D. walked to the small front porch of Ruby's house and picked up a small duffle bag that was on the step. Ruby stood on the porch above him. She wore a t-shirt that didn't quite hang down far enough to cover the more than ample cheeks of her bare butt. It was obvious she wore nothing underneath the thin cotton shirt. Johnny D. scanned her body and stepped up onto the porch next to her, dropping the bag back on the step. He moved Ruby back into the house and to the couch in her living room, where he pulled off her t-shirt exposing her incredible female attributes. She stood there naked. She was used to that. Johnny D. pulled his pants down to his boots and sat down on the couch with his manhood standing at attention for her. Ruby knelt down on the floor at his feet and he pulled her head down into his lap as the dogs started barking.

"You make me and the dogs crazy, woman."

* * *

There would be a marker placed in the Mayport cemetery for Jimmy Johnson, but there was no burial. It was another sad day in the little fishing village of Mayport, Florida, U.S.A. Mr. King had not returned from his trip to Gibsonton, Florida, but with no body, they did not need to use his Classic Cadillac hearse anyway.

The police cars and other vehicles were leaving the churchyard as Mr. Leek stepped out of the front of the church. Hawk, Jason and Mary C. were at the walkway below the steps. Mary C. held Billy in her arms. Hawk saw Mr. Leek first.

"Ya did the young man real proud in there, Al. Ya said the right things."

"Thank ya, Hawk. That was the hardest thing I've had to do in a long time." Mr. Leek looked at Jason. They both knew nothing could compare to the day Mr. Leek killed Jake and saved Jessie at the sand hill under the oak tree, but that was a secret forever. Jason saw Miss Margaret and her four daughters crossing the front churchyard toward their family station wagon. He wanted to see Sofia, but he knew he would have to talk to the other three girls and he wasn't ready for that. Mary C. stopped to show the baby to the older Peggy as Hawk and Mr. Leek walked to Hawk's truck. Mr. Leek took a deep breath.

"I stood right there, Hawk. I couldn't save him. I thought I had him and then he was gone. It looked like slow motion, and still it happened so fast. I can't explain it, but I'll never forget it." Hawk took his own deep breath.

"Mary C. said there was nothin' anyone could do. You did save the boy. And that's what Jimmy was trying to do. He was a brave young man and he knew the risk he was takin' when he went in after the boy. In his mind and heart at that moment, he had no other choice."

Mr. Leek nodded, but he was still sad and frustrated about the death of his young fishing buddy. Older Peggy looked at Mary C.'s grandson, Billy, for a few seconds, but she was more interested in Mary C.'s son, Jason.

"How's Jason doin'? I haven't seen him since he got back. And how are you doin'? I heard about your awful ordeal with those voodoo people. But, I also heard you kicked quite a bit of voodoo ass in the process." Peggy did have a way with words. Her Southern accent and drawl were classic. Mary C. had to smile at Peggy's statement, mainly because Peggy was the first one to speak the truth about that night. Mary C. liked the thought of "kickin' ass."

"We're both doin' fine, Peggy. Thanks for askin'."

"Mama calls you two the Mayport survivors. She says there ain't nothin' you two can't handle. She does love you and that son of yours." Mary C. liked the way older Peggy talked. The always aggressive and sexy older Peggy had her head on a swivel looking for Jason. A huge smile covered her face when Mary C. pointed Jason out in the crowd. Older Peggy kissed Mary C. on her cheek and went to find her sex man who had thrown her off the mountain.

Mr. Leek and Hawk both looked toward Mayport Road as a white Mercedes Benz drove slowly past the church. Hawk didn't recognize the driver. Mr. Leek did.

"I thought he was gone. I don't like him bein' around here. He ain't got no reason to be hangin' around. He ain't got no good reason for stayin' here. I smell trouble when I'm around him." Hawk didn't recognize the Punjabi priest and he didn't understand Mr. Leek's concern.

"Who is it?"

"It's that Indian fella Eve brought here. You know, the holy man with the tattoos and long hair."

Hawk's heart raced in his chest as the vision of the warrior flashed in his head. "That wasn't him drivin' that car. That's not the same car's been at the King house."

"That's the same car and that's him. He just looks different without that long hair or that rag on his head. I saw him at Margaret's store flirtin' with the young one, Sofia. That's him all right. I don't like him one bit."

"You saw him at the store and he cut all his hair off?"

"That's right. That's why ya didn't recognize him. He really looks different. I don't like him talkin' to those young girls. It ain't none of my business, but I don't want them girls to get hurt. He's the kind would talk one into goin' off somewhere with him. He might even steal one of 'em and use her as a slave or somethin' even worse. People from other countries do crazy things and they don't care. They still have slaves in some of those wild countries and he looks like the slavin' kind. I asked him when he was leavin' and he said 'soon.' That was four days ago. That don't sound like soon to me." The white Mercedes was gone from their sight. Mr. Leek had some more interesting information about the Punjabi priest for Hawk to absorb.

"He said he had lost something and had to find it before he could leave, but he didn't say what it was. He left the store when I started questioning him." The sight of the Kirpan sword flashed in Hawk's head. He understood. Mary C. joined Hawk and Mr. Leek.

"Miss Margaret and her girls want me and Billy to ride

with them. The girls want to see Billy. Hey, Al. Your talk was nice." Mr. Leek nodded and Mary C. walked away with Billy in her arms. She didn't need permission from Hawk, she was just telling him what she was doing.

Older Peggy had located Jason as he moved between one of the small buildings in the churchyard. Even though the yard was still crowded the building was rather isolated. She was prepared for a moment alone with her one time, year ago, and now favorite lover.

"Jason, how are you!"

Jason turned to see her hurry to him. "Hey, Peggy. I'm fine."

She threw her arms around him and pressed her huge hard breasts against his muscular chest. "Isn't this just awful?" Jason patted her on her back as she continued pushing her pelvic area through his. "Where have you been? I have missed you so much. I think about you all the time. And you have a son. You have been busy. And your mama saved the baby from the voodoo people. Betty left town with a man. She thinks she's in love. I'm in that big house and that big bed all alone. Is this world crazy or what?" Peggy had more information than Jason was ready to absorb. She knew their time was limited and she wanted to say as much as she could in a short amount of time. At Jason's urging she released her hold on him. "Please come see me soon. Betty's gone. Your Uncle Bobby's gone. You've been gone. All these people dyin'. Life's just too short to miss out on the good things. And you are one of the good things, Jason. Don't pass me up. Come see me, please. I promise you won't regret it." Jason nodded and older Peggy kissed him on his lips and touched him between his legs. "Y'all come see me, ya hear?"

Jason left older Peggy by the small building and stepped out into the open. He saw his mother and Billy getting into Miss

Margaret's family station wagon. Sofia reached from the back seat and took Billy from Mary C. Margie was sitting in the front seat on the passenger's side. Jason could see the sadness on her face. The car moved away as Hawk stepped up behind Jason.

"Ya mama went with Miss Margaret. You goin' with me? I'm gonna go to the boat and clean that hold out. I gotta change of clothes on the boat."

"Yes sir, I do, too."

*   *   *

The black El Camino with the six Rottweilers in the back drove away from Ruby's house. She could hear the truck move away as she lay naked on the couch. She cried out loud at the fact that her purpose was to keep the devil man sexually satisfied. She didn't like that thought, but she didn't like the thought of being fed to the devil dogs either.

*   *   *

Mr. John King sat on the edge of his bed in one of the cottages at the Giant's Motel in Gibsonton, Florida. The beautiful and voluptuous belly dancer, Ana Kara, stood across the room. She was dressed in her authentic Turkish belly dancer attire. There was a small box type record player on the table next to the bed. The exotic sounds of the Middle Eastern music came from the box and filled the small room. Ana's nimble fingers moved her zills and the small metal finger cymbals added to the music coming from the single speaker of the record player. The music consisted of the flute sounds of the ney, the oboe sounds of the zurna and the beating of the doumbek drums. Ana moved her body to the strange and delightful beat as John sat watching. It would be the night Mr. John King would have his own private belly dancer. It was a first in his life.

* * *

Hawk and Jason were cleaning the hold of the boat. Al Leek was home with his family. Mr. Butler was having a drink at Smitty's in Jacksonville Beach. Mary C. walked up onto her front porch carrying her grandson, Billy, as Miss Margaret and her four daughters drove away in their family station wagon. Mary C. had not seen the white Mercedes parked in the woods near the road leading to her house. She held Billy in one arm and unlocked the door with her other hand. Mary C. stopped turning the key in the lock when she realized she was not alone on the porch. Her peripheral vision had revealed to her that someone was standing on the porch at the left side of the house. She turned slowly to face the unwanted intruder. When Mary C. saw a big baldheaded man standing there, she did not recognize Sandeep. She turned the lock quickly, pushed the door open and moved into the house with Billy. Sandeep moved to the door as Mary C. slammed it shut.

"I've got a gun in here and I will use it!" Mary C. placed Billy on the floor next to the couch and grabbed her pump action shotgun that was placed strategically behind the door. With one confident motion she pulled down the pump handle on the gun and chambered one of the shells. "I don't want to hurt you, mister, but I will." Sandeep stepped away from the door and into the front yard, just in case she started shooting. He thought moving away would help her see him better and he would be able to talk before she pulled the trigger.

"I mean no harm to you or the child. I am Sandeep Singh and I only wish to talk to you."

Mary C. looked out the front window and pointed the gun at him so he would know she meant business. Sandeep was surprised when she moved away from the window and walked out of the house with the shotgun pointed directly at him. He backed up even more.

"I will kill you where you stand, mister. Now, get out of my yard."

"Please allow me to speak before you shoot me. I will stand at this distance if you permit it."

Mary C. recognized him. "You're that Indian man stayin' at John's house, ain't ya? Ya look different."

"I am Sandeep Singh. I am a holy man. I have come to ask you to make the one they call Hawk return the holy Kirpan so I can leave this place." Mary C. knew he was referring to the big knife Hawk had taken from him after their fight.

"You really look different without that thing on your head."

"I will be this way until I have recovered the Kirpan."

"You need to get off my property. I've already talked to you too long. I usually don't do that."

Sandeep didn't want to reveal himself to her, but he knew it was the only way to reach her.

"I was with you the night you fought for the golden child. The Kirpan sliced clean and deep."

Mary C.'s eyes opened wide. She lowered the gun. "What did you say?"

"I was here with you that night. We fought as one. You just did not know it."

"You're Singin' Sandy, ain't ya? You're the one the old voodoo woman told me about.

"I am Sandeep Singh."

"Same thing."

Sandeep had more to shock Mary C.

"I thought I was a slave forever, but you set me free when

you defeated the one who held me. It was only right the fire should consume her."

Mary C. lowered the gun to her side and opened the front door. "You ain't gonna hurt us, are ya?"

"I can only protect the child. It is my duty as a Punjabi. You protect yourself. You need no one. It is a privilege and honor to be here with you."

Mary C. remained cautious, but she wanted to talk to the mysterious man. "You come sit on the steps." Mary C. stepped out onto the porch and moved to one of the chairs and sat down with the shotgun in her lap. The barrel was still pointing in Sandeep's direction. He sat on one of the steps.

"I am sorry I frightened you. That was not my intent."

Mary C. had to know. "Why were you here that night?"

"I came to see the child. I wanted to see if he was golden like the one called Sofia had said."

"Sofia told you he was a golden child?"

"She said he was of the tree and had powers. She did not use the word golden. When I came here you were at war and it is my duty to protect you. I am a warrior."

"Why didn't I see you? Why didn't you tell me?"

"There was no need. What would be the reason?"

"So I could thank you properly for saving our lives."

"You repaid me ten times over when you set me free." Mary C. knew he meant Eve's timely death. She would not ask him any more questions about that night. She was an expert at keeping secrets burned deep in her beautiful belly. It was time to change the subject. Sandeep did the honors.

"I have come for the Kirpan sword. I pray you will give it to me."

"Your jaw looks painful."

"It will not be so when the Kirpan is returned."

Mary C. had to be Mary C. "Hawk broke your jaw and took your knife, didn't he?"

"Yes. He was a most formidable opponent."

Mary C. liked the way that sounded. She nodded her head as if she knew what formidable meant. Sandeep and Mary C. turned when they heard the sound of a truck motor coming down the road to her house. It was Hawk and Jason returning from the dock. Hawk jumped out of the truck when it stopped near the steps. Sandeep stood up quickly. Hawk looked at Mary C., holding the shotgun.

"You all right, Mary C.?" Hawk stepped toward the Indian. Mary C. yelled.

"I'm fine! Don't hurt him!" Sandeep did not take a defensive stance as Hawk came closer to him. Mary C. yelled again. "He ain't done nothin' wrong. He came to get the knife." Hawk stopped his advance as Jason joined him. Sandeep bowed his head.

"I mean no disrespect or harm to you. I am ashamed of my actions against you. I will never be able to change my shame. Please forgive me. I am glad I was not able to defeat you. It is an honor to be here with you." Hawk looked at Mary C. She said, "Give him his knife," with her eyes. Hawk nodded and Mary C. went into the house. Sandeep had to speak to Jason.

"You are most special, but you are losing your way. You must find it before it is too late for you. You may have to leave this place to do so." Mary C. interrupted Sandeep's comments to Jason when she walked back out onto the porch holding the Kirpan sword in her arms. Sandeep's face lit up as much as it could with a broken jaw. Mary C. handed the holy relic to the Punjabi priest. He took it and bowed his baldhead to her. He turned and bowed to Hawk and Jason.

"I will leave this strange place, now. I have remained here

too long. I have gained more than I have lost here. I must go home to complete my cleansing." The bald headed Punjabi turned and walked out of the yard and into the woods where he had left the white Mercedes Benz. Hawk, Jason and Mary C. went into the house.

CHAPTER EIGHT

MR. BUTLER SAT ON A BAR STOOL IN SMITTY'S BAR NEAR THE OCEAN in Jacksonville Beach. He could hear the music from the board-walk amusement rides and the noise of the people enjoying all the excitement. The usual screams from the Wild Mouse roller coaster were silent. The popular scary ride had been discontin-ued after the car went off the track and two young sailors died. Mr. Butler turned to see two uniformed police officers walking toward him. He recognized his loyal fellow officers, Paul Short and David Boos, as they came closer to the bar.

"Hey, men. Come on and join me in a toast to our good friend and dumb ass, Jimmy Johnston." The two officers knew their boss and good friend was sad and mad about the death of the well-liked Jimmy Johnston. They were there to help. Paul Short stepped up to the bar next to Mr. Butler.

"Can we give you a ride home, sir?" Mr. Butler held his empty rock glass up to Paul and David. His speech was slurred.

"To Officer Jimmy Johnston. I loved that boy." He held his head down for a second and then lifted it quickly. "He knew to stay away from her and he still took her with him. I wonder how she got him to do that? Oh, and let's drink to that beautiful angel of death who lays in waiting for us all. How does she know to be there when they die?" Paul and David took Mr. Butler's arms and escorted him to their patrol car. They knew he was in mourning.

* * *

Margie lay on her bed staring up at the ceiling above her. Sofia slowly opened the door to the room and looked in. "Are you sleeping?"

Margie looked at Sofia. "No. Come in." Sofia moved to the bed and sat down next to her oldest sister.

"I told mother I'd check on you. You all right?"

"No, I'm not." Sofia bowed her head and allowed her older sister to continue. "I'm sick about Jimmy. It was awful. But, you know that. You were there, too." Sofia held her head down. Margie needed to talk and she surprised Sofia when she took her hand. Sofia looked up to see Margie's eyes fill with tears.

"You are so good to me all the time, Sofia. We have kept each other's secrets. I gave the music box to Mary C." Sofia's eyes lit up. "Don't be angry. Let them battle with it. It would have done something to us and you know that." Sofia nodded her head in agreement as Margie dropped the bomb.

"I think I'm carrying Jimmy's baby."

* * *

Susan looked out the door of the store when the white Mercedes stopped in front. The bald-headed Sandeep Singh stepped out of the car and entered the store, ringing the bell as he pushed the door open. Susan was afraid, but she gave the official greeting.

"Good afternoon. May I help you with something?"

"Is the one called Sofia here?" Susan hesitated as the Punjabi approached the counter.

"No sir, she already worked today."

"Will you tell her something for me?"

"Yes, sir."

"Tell her it was a great honor to have seen her and I hope we meet again in this life or another. Will you tell her that?'

"Yes, sir, I will." The Punjabi was out the door and into the Mercedes. As the luxury car drove away from the store, another white vehicle drove up to the front of Mr. King's haunted house. The classic white Cadillac hearse stopped in the front yard. Mr. King had returned from his trip to Gibsonton, Florida and his visit to the Giant's Motel. He was glad to be back in his hometown of Mayport.

* * *

The black El Camino drove onto the ferry from the Fort George side of the river. Johnny D. Bryant, the Ax, and his six devil dogs would be in Mayport in about fifteen minutes. No one in Mayport knew it yet, but a new evil was coming to town with bad intentions and six trained-to-kill Rottweilers. Sandeep Singh sat in his white Mercedes waiting for the ferry to return to the Mayport side of the river. He would cross on the ferry and drive North up the seacoast. His destination was New York and a plane to Afghanistan.

* * *

Sofia sat on Margie's bed in disbelief. "Are you sure, Margie?"

"Well, I'm pretty sure. I don't know much about it, but there's something different in me and I haven't had a monthly in two months. And you know I never miss that joyous occasion."

Sofia forced a smile. "If it's true what will you do? What will Mother do? What will Father do?"

Margie rolled her eyes. "Father probably won't even notice or care for that matter. He hasn't been here for any of us including Mother. Who cares what he thinks? Mother's a different story."

"Do you think Mother will send you away? They sent that girl, Julia, away when it happened to her. I heard Mother talking about it."

"Sofia, that girl was fifteen years old. I'm twenty-two. No one can send me away. Now, I could just go away to save Mother the embarrassment."

"Oh, please don't leave us, Margie! I couldn't bear it here without you to tell me what is best for me."

"Sofia, you are so silly and so dramatic. You sound like one of those young girls in those sword fighting movies. You must promise me you will never tell this unless I tell it first. Promise me."

"I promise."

* * *

Jason walked into the living room where Hawk and Mary C. were sitting. "I'm gonna take a ride if you don't need me. I might go get something to eat out at Bill's Hideaway." Mary C. smiled. She liked the thought of being alone with Hawk.

"I'll leave the porch light on for ya." Jason nodded to his mother, smiled and left the house. Mary C. moved next to Hawk on the couch.

"I'm glad you're home tonight. I need to release some of this energy boilin' up inside of me. I'd like to release the fury on you."

Hawk was always amazed at Mary C.'s aggressive

nature, but he loved it when he was the recipient of her favors.

"I'd like that, too. You do have a way of sayin' things to take a person's mind off his worries. It's like magic."

"I thought you didn't believe in magic."

"I believe in your magic." Mary C.'s eyes lit up. She couldn't believe Hawk had said that.

"You think I'm like magic, Hawk? You don't mean like a witch, do ya?"

Hawk shook his head and smiled. "No. I don't think that. It's when we make love. Bells really do ring in my head. Magic bells." Mary C. had never seen that side of Hawk. It was different and romantic. It was his way of giving her a compliment. She thought about something important she had to say.

"You are a man's man, Hawk. And you're a woman's man. That ain't easy to be." Hawk wasn't sure where Mary C. was going with the "man's man, woman's man" philosophy. He would listen before he responded. Mary C. went on. "There ain't many real men around, ya know. Men like you, I mean. You fight if ya have to. You help folks when they need it. You work hard. You can defeat a warrior and take his sword and the next day you can rub a horny toad's belly and make it sleep for those silly little girls. There ain't many like you, Lester Hawkins, and I'm glad you're here with me." She kissed Hawk with a kiss that could only be the prelude to the Mary C. sexual mo-jo. Hawk recognized the style. "You go on and get in the shower. I need to check on Billy. I'll join you in just a minute." Hawk didn't hesitate. He stood up to follow her request. Mary C. turned to Hawk as she moved toward the hall.

"Thanks, Hawk."

"For what?"

"For not saying nothing about how you warned me about

going to that awful place. I won't ever say that word again."

"Good." Hawk walked to the bathroom and started the shower. Mary C. checked on Billy.

* * *

Jason walked up the stairs to the front door of Bill's Hideaway. He stopped and looked at the place on the railing where he had cut off two of Charlie Klim's fingers. He moved on from the unpleasant memory and pushed open the two swinging doors that lead to the main dining room of the best honky tonk in the immediate vicinity. The aroma of hushpuppies cooking filled the air. The music was loud and heavy rock-n-roll, the dance floor was full of beach boppers and jitter buggers and the pool balls were cracking. It sounded like the Croom twins were throwing raw eggs at the Mayport schoolhouse windows.

Jason looked out at the dance floor and saw older Peggy turning and twisting across the hardwood floor. She saw him at the same time and danced away from her partner and danced in front of Jason. He had experienced the joy of having women dance for him before. He had always liked it. Peggy was as sexy as she could be. She moved back to her dance partner for the rest of the song, but her sights were on Jason.

* * *

Mary C. stood behind Hawk and rubbed a bar of soap over his back and buttocks. He stood there as the water from the shower bounced off his chest. She moved around in front of him and washed his erect manliness as the water bounced off her back. Mary C. handed Hawk the bar of soap.

"Your turn." Hawk took the soap and moved the wet bar

over Mary C.'s breasts and stomach. As the lather increased he moved his hand between her legs and pushed water, lather and two of his fingers inside her. She opened her legs for more pleasure and a deeper cleaning. Hawk obliged her and added a finger.

Mary C. turned her back to her washman. Hawk lathered her up and moved the bar of soap up and down between her butt cheeks. Mary C. bent forward and put her hands on the wall of the shower as Hawk found another spot for one of his wet and soapy fingers. Mary C. moaned as Hawk added a second finger. They would both be squeaky clean before the erotic shower ended.

*   *   *

Officers David Boos and Paul Short sat with Mr. Butler in his living room. Mr. Butler took a cup of coffee down from his lips.

"I really appreciate you two getting me home. Folks don't need to see me out there drinkin' like that. This thing with Jimmy has just drained me. I wish I had known she was going with him." The two officers were ready to listen to Mr. Butler until he was completely sober. "You know she's gotten away with killin' a lot of people. People die around her all the time. She's the angel of death and she keeps on doin' it. Now, she did it to Jimmy."

*   *   *

Hawk walked to the bedroom with a towel wrapped around his lower body. Mary C. walked behind him totally naked. She picked up the magic carousel as they passed it in the living room. Hawk moved to the bed as Mary C. placed the music box on the small table next to the bed. Hawk saw the carousel and shook his head as he dropped the towel on the floor and got into the bed. Mary C.'s squeaky clean naked body was all he cared about at that moment. He didn't need a magic music box. He had Mary C.

Mary C. pushed the small lever on the carousel and crawled into the bed like a wildcat after its prey. The music started to play and the multi-colored light began to twinkle and bounce off the ceiling and walls of the room. Hawk looked into Mary C.'s eyes as she sat across him. The hundred flashing lights had found their way into her eyes and the combination of the magic music box and the Mary C. mo-jo would be too much for a mere mortal man. Hawk was a man's man.

* * *

The ferry had docked on the Mayport side of the river. The front of the big floating carrier had been secured and the five vehicles that had boarded on the Fort George side were rolling off the ferry and into Mayport.

Sandeep was standing outside his car in the fresh air as the cars moved past him. The last vehicle was the black El Camino with the Ax at the wheel and the six dogs in the back. For some reason, Sandeep's eyes met the black eyes of Johnny D. Bryant. The Punjabi knew a soldier of Satan had passed by him. There was no doubt in Sandeep's mind that there was an evil presence as the truck went by and he saw the dogs in their cages. The dogs went wild, barking, growling and showing their teeth in disrespect for the holy man. Sandeep got into his car and drove onto the ferry. It was time for the priest to leave Mayport to do its own battle with the evils of the world.

* * *

Hawk knew he was having sexual relations with Mary C., but he felt like she was more than one woman. She was many women. He could feel her mouth on his manliness, but she was kissing his lips at the same time. He saw her above him with her head thrown back with pleasure, yet he felt her hard hot breasts against his back. He knew he was inside her, yet her hand was pulling the fluids from his body. He knew he had exploded to end the passion, yet he was big again as if he had just started. He didn't know it, but Mary C. was experiencing the same sensations.

She felt Hawk deep inside her, yet his tongue touched her at the same time. At one time she felt him kissing her on both sets of her lips. She knew he entered her from behind, and yet she was looking into his eyes at the same time. The two lovers did the work of ten until the carousel stopped spinning, the music went silent and the lights no longer flashed in Mary C.'s eyes or off the walls. The ten were gone. Only the two spent and exhausted lovers remained. They were not sleeping. They were unconscious.

* * *

Jason lay with older Peggy in her boat bed. She was on her stomach next to him. He had just thrown her off that sexual mountain she had wanted to climb for over a year. Older Peggy was in the recovery mode and she was preparing for a full night of incredible sex with her old boyfriend's nephew. Jason didn't realize when they talked at the church that he would have accepted her invitation within a few hours. Older Peggy had joined Mary C. and Hawk in the post-sexual condition of unconsciousness. Jason went to her icebox in search of a Nehi.

* * *

Ruby stepped to the small window of her front door to see who was knocking. "Who is it?"

"It's me, Miss Ruby, Banjo." She opened the door and let him into the house. As usual, Ruby was scantly dressed. She had her t-shirt on and you could see through it if the light hit her at the right angle. She had panties on under the shirt, but that was all. Banjo had to swallow in order to talk.

"I'm sorry to bother you again, Miss Ruby, but I think I dropped my paycheck here last time. I had it in my shirt pocket and I've looked everywhere. I've backtracked all the places I went and this is my last hope. It was folded up and I think when I was leaving in such a hurry, I dropped it. Could I look around and kind'a follow where I went when I was here?"

"Of course. I haven't seen it, but you can look anywhere you like. I hope it's here somewhere."

"Thank ya ma'am." Banjo went out to the back porch first. Ruby didn't follow him. She walked into her front room and turned on the radio. Jackie Wilson's rock-n-roll gem, "Work Out" blasted from the small black box.

Banjo heard the music as he stepped out onto the back porch. Banjo stood in the same spot where he trembled in fear before. He looked down at the wooden slats of the porch floor. There were two slats with a wider separation than the others. He knelt down and peered through the opening to the ground below and there it was. His folded paper paycheck had fallen through the opening and had been under Ruby's back porch. He walked down the steps and crawled under the porch on his hands and knees until he reached it. He couldn't turn around, but he was able to back out slowly from under Ruby's porch.

Jackie Wilson was shouting, "Baby work out," as Banjo made his way back down the hall and to the front of the house.

He stopped dead in his tracks when he saw Ruby dancing in the room. Her huge breasts and her bubble butt bounced all over as she jumped around the room. When she turned and saw him watching her, she didn't miss a beat. She liked it when men watched her dance. Banjo held up his check and raised his voice above the music.

"I found it under the porch. Can I wash my hands?" Ruby nodded and kept dancing. Banjo moved to the bathroom he had passed in the hall. He put the check in his front pocket of his pants and turned the water on in the sink. He washed the dirt off his hands and forearms. The Jackie Wilson song ended, but he heard Little Richard's "Long Tall Sally" rock the house. Banjo's heart raced in his chest when he looked into the bathroom mirror above the sink. Ruby was dancing in the doorway. He got nervous when he saw her.

"Miss Ruby, you might just be the prettiest woman God has made."

She smiled at his surprising compliment. "Take a shower with me, Banjo."

"I'm scared Miss Ruby. You scare me. The Ax scares me. The dogs scare me."

"He won't be back. I won't tell on ya, I promise." Ruby took off her shirt and panties and stepped naked into the bathtub. Banjo couldn't believe what was happening. She pulled the shower curtain closed and turned on the water.

"I ain't got no hot water, but you'll get used to it. Come on in." Banjo's clothes hit the floor and he pulled the curtain back enough to allow himself enough room to climb into the shower with the black beauty. Ruby held a bar of soap in her hand. There would be squeaky clean white folks in Mayport and black folks in Cosmos.

"When we're both clean I will pleasure you like you have

never been pleasured before. I expect to be paid for my favors and efforts."

"The only money I've got is that paycheck, but I can pay you when I get it cashed." She reached down and took his manhood in her hand.

"I don't want your money. I want you to tell me what Johnny D.'s planning to do. Why did you come here for him?" She turned the shower off, reached for a towel and stepped out of the bathtub. She dried her wet body and handed Banjo a towel. "I'll be in my room if you want me." She left the bathroom. Banjo dried quickly, picked up his clothes and went to her room. He stopped dead in his tracks again when he saw Ruby wet, naked and spread-eagle on her bed. It was only a matter of time for Ruby to have all the information she wanted. Banjo would be singing like a canary.

The black El Camino truck drove up to a cinder block house located near the Blue Moon Tavern. The Ax stepped out of the truck and was greeted by Macadoo as she came out the front door.

"I knew you'd come. I'm sorry 'bout ya mama." He followed the fat woman into her house. Nighttime had come to Mayport.

CHAPTER NINE

THE MORNING SUN IN MAYPORT TOUCHED JASON'S FACE THROUGH an opening in the window curtain of his bedroom. He had made it home from his evening with older Peggy and he could feel the results of their second sexual encounter. Jason wasn't sure why he had gone home with her, he just had. Mary C. and Hawk would not wake up for hours and it would take them both the entire day to recover from the effects of the magic carousel.

* * *

Sofia had been up, off and on, during the night, praying for Margie and thinking about her oldest sister's predicament. Margie was throwing up in the bathroom from a touch of morning sickness and the toll of the last few days leading up to Jimmy's funeral. Sofia heard Margie, but didn't go to comfort her.

* * *

Mr. King sat on his front porch drinking a cup of coffee. He was glad to be home. He waved at Peggy as she got out of the family station wagon to relieve her sister, Susan, at the store.

Susan got into the wagon and Miss Margaret turned back toward home. She stopped the car in front of Mr. King's house and rolled down the driver's side window.

"Welcome home, John. I hope you had a safe trip. I'm sorry about the death of the young woman."

"Thank you, Margaret. The trip was fine."

"Did you hear about Jimmy Johnston?" She knew by the look on his face he knew nothing about Jimmy's death.

"No. What is it?"

Miss Margaret pressed her lips together. "He got killed. That fine young man is dead." Mr. King's heart moved to his throat.

"Oh my God, Margaret. Somebody shoot him?"

"No, John. It was awful. He jumped into the gator pit at the Gator Farm to save one of his boys and the gators killed him, right there in front of everybody. My three girls were there. It's just awful." Mr. King was sick to his stomach. "I'll talk to you later, John." He nodded as Miss Margaret drove away.

*   *   *

Macadoo sat at her breakfast table with Johnny D. Bryant. "I didn't hear one of your dogs bark last night. Out of all them dogs, not one made a noise during the night."

"They had no reason."

"Are you sure tonight is the right time? You don't think you should wait?"

"You sent for me because you know it has to be done and you know I am the one. What difference does it make when it happens? I know Voo Swar will not rest until she greets this woman in hell."

"The oak baby's still there. I have felt the power in the

child. Voo Swar knew of the child's power, too. We must consider that."

"I will cook and eat this child, if it will get me to the woman." Macadoo didn't like his disrespect for the power of the oak baby, but she understood it. She knew Voo Swar did not believe in the tree, yet she also knew Voo Swar wanted the child. It was a true contradiction.

"I have others to help you end her reign of death. They are willing to go with you if you will allow it. They are the kinfolk of the ones who have died at her hand."

The Ax looked at Macadoo. "I will only take six with me."

*   *   *

John King and Al Leek walked out of Mr. King's house and stood on the porch.

"Thank you, Al, for coming by and telling me about Jimmy. I heard the sad news from Margaret, but I didn't pursue the details. This is truly a horrible thing. He is a true hero."

Mr. Leek changed the subject. "How was your trip down South?"

Mr. King smiled. "It was interesting. That's the best word to describe it—interesting. I'll tell you all about it when you have the time. Those circus folks are really somethin' else."

Mr. Leek nodded and smiled. "You seem to fit right in with 'em, John. And I know you're not gonna tell me everything."

Mr. King smiled a big grin. "You're right about that."

*   *   *

Hawk sat on the edge of the bed. Mary C. was still asleep next to him. She was also still naked. Hawk pulled the sheet up and placed it over her. He looked at the now still and quiet carousel. He knew something had happened, but he wasn't exactly sure what it was. Hawk did not want to believe in magic. He knew there had to be a rational explanation for the unbelievable night of sex, dreams and hallucinations he had experienced. Hawk heard Jason in the kitchen, so he stood up on weak legs, put his pants on and went to join Jason. Jason was at the table.

"Good mornin', Jason."

"Mornin'."

"How was Bill's last night?"

"Fine. Good crowd." Older Peggy's naked body flashed in Jason's head. He would keep his night with her a secret. Hawk was puzzled.

"Jason, do you think if you tell somebody that something will happen, the person can get it in their mind and make it happen in their mind? You know, like it didn't really happen, but you think it did?" Jason looked at Hawk. It was too early for Jason to cipher Hawk's philosophy riddle so he took a few seconds to respond to the question. Hawk couldn't wait. "I think they call it the 'power of suggestion'. Yeah, that's it. You suggest somethin' to the person and they make it happen in their head." It was time for Jason to make his response.

"Mama turned on the music box, didn't she?"

*   *   *

Ruby stepped out of a car at the ferry slip on the Fort George side of the river. She closed the car door and waved good-bye to the driver as the car drove away. She would catch the ferry to Mayport. Banjo had shared in her favors and he shared his knowledge of what was to come. She wanted to see her friend Jessie's child: the one Banjo called "oak baby."

Mr. Butler sat at his desk in his office at the Atlantic Beach Police Station. Officers Paul Short and David Boos walked in. "Mornin', men. I need to thank you two again for getting me home last night. Your efforts on my behalf were far beyond your normal duty. I appreciate your help." Paul nodded. David replied.

"You're welcome, sir. It was a sad day." Mr. Butler pressed his lips together. Paul had interesting information.

"Your Indian man hightailed it out of town. He took the ferry out of Mayport and headed North." It was music to Mr. Butler's ears.

"Good. That's another crazy gone. The circus left, the woman left and now he's gone. If I could get rid of the Mayport black widow angel of death we wouldn't have any work to do." He looked angry. "You know, I knew it was just a matter of time before she got Jimmy. He just couldn't stay away from that Margie girl. And that girl started spendin' too much time with that woman. Jimmy couldn't see it comin'. The more he went to Mayport to see that girl, the closer he got to Mary C. Why is it that she is always around when people die? It would take all day for me to go over the list of folks who have died with her within shoutin' distance; some at her hand and others just close to her. You know she fought like a man when those voodoo people attacked her house?" The two officers nodded. They knew the story.

*   *   *

Ruby walked off the ferry on the Mayport side of the river. She looked up and saw the great oak tree towering above the sand hill. She walked toward the great tree looking for the oak baby.

A small army of six black men had gathered in Macadoo's back yard. The six devil dogs lay on the ground in a circle around the Ax. He sat in silence as Macadoo addressed the six men.

"Has anyone seen Banjo? He's supposed to be here."

One of the men spoke up. "I was to pick him up on my way here. He wasn't home. I asked the old man next door if he had seen him and he told me he saw Banjo leave early this mornin'. His car was packed like he would be gone for a while. Looks like he decided not to do this."

Macadoo was surprised, but continued. "You all know why we are here. After tonight we will not speak of this again. You are all here of your own free will and may leave if you do not wish to stay. Go now before the Ax speaks to you." All six heads turned to the Ax. No one talked. No one left.

* * *

Margie stood at the oak tree. She wasn't sure why she had gone there: perhaps to be alone, perhaps to clear her head of all that pounded her brain. She was afraid of what was to become of her, now that she carried Jimmy's child inside her. She would have to wait to have Jason's oak baby. Margie was obsessed with the concept of being the mother of an oak baby. Perhaps she was hoping the tree would give her the answers to her dilemma. Perhaps she wanted to rub herself against the tree as she had done before. Whatever the reason, she stood next to the huge trunk of the Mayport oak tree.

* * *

Mary C. walked into the kitchen wearing her white terry cloth bathrobe. "Good mornin', you two. How 'bout some

French toast?" Mary C. seemed to always make a connection with sex, death and French toast.

* * *

The Ax stood in the center of his circle of dogs. He was an intimidating sight for the six men who had joined Macadoo's plan of revenge. It was obvious to all present, including Macadoo, that Johnny D. Bryant was totally insane. His years with the voodoo queen, Voo Swar, had convinced him he was the son of the devil and he was protected as a true prince of darkness. Macadoo also knew she needed such a man to defeat Mary C. and her companions. It didn't matter to Macadoo what instrument of revenge she had to use. If it took insane, so be it. They were all quiet as they waited for the Ax to speak.

"It's hard for me to believe that one white woman has caused such grief and havoc with you and your families. She has also taken from me and she has left my loved one with no way to cross over. Her death will set many free."

* * *

The house smelled like French toast. Jason was eating the last piece of the egg covered sweet bread. Hawk sat in the living room looking at the Times-Union newspaper. Mary C. put the last dish in the clean dish rack. She looked at Jason.

"You wash that dish when you're finished."

"Yes, Ma'am." Mary C. left the kitchen and walked into the living room with Hawk. She turned the radio on. The sound of the song "Shotgun" by Junior Walker and the All Stars came blaring out of the radio. "Shotgun...Shoot 'em for they run now." Mary C. turned to Hawk as the song continued. "Do the jerk, baby. Do the jerk, now." She danced to him.

"Have you heard this song? Listen to this song. It might be

my new favorite. It's called 'Shotgun'. Neat, huh?" Hawk put the paper down.

"And this is your new favorite song?"

"Yeah, I think so. It's a great dance song. Don't ya think? And don't tell me that Lester Hawkins don't know a good dance song when he hears one." She danced closer to Hawk. He smiled and had a thought.

"Maybe if you sing about a shotgun, you won't have to carry one around."

"Maybe if folks would leave me alone I wouldn't have to have one at my side all the time." The song continued as Mary C. danced off to her bedroom. She was gone for a few seconds and then she looked back from the bedroom door to get Hawk's attention. Hawk looked up to see Mary C. at the door showing him half of her naked body: one leg, one breast, one eye. Hawk's eyes widened when he saw her enticing display. She gave a half smile.

"You believe in magic now, don't ya?"

* * *

Margie touched the trunk of the oak with her hand and started walking around the tree. She had almost completed a full circle when she stopped and saw a young black woman standing at the edge of the sand hill.

"Oh, my! You scared me!" Ruby stepped back.

"I'm sorry. I didn't see you, either." They stared at each other for a few seconds.

"I'm Margie."

"I'm Ruby. I've heard about this tree, but I've never seen it. You live here?"

"Unfortunately, I must say yes."

Ruby smiled. "Is living here a bad thing?"

"Let's just say, it smells like fish all the time." Ruby smiled again and looked up into the tree.

"The tree is beautiful, ain't it? My best friend loved this tree. In fact she was what they call a believer in the tree. Her mother was killed here."

Margie was intrigued. "What's your friend's name?"

"Jessie. Jessie Brown, but she's dead. She died havin' a baby." Margie tried not to react to the information from the beautiful black stranger, who just happened to visit the tree for the first time while Margie was there. Margie knew the tree had caused it to happen. Ruby knew Margie had recognized Jessie's name.

"I'm lookin' for Jessie's son. I heard her baby lives here. I would love to see her baby. She was like a sister to me. I feel like I'm the child's aunt. Do you know of the child?"

Margie's face said, "yes". Ruby was excited.

"You have heard of the child. Please tell me what you know." Margie couldn't believe she was standing at the tree with a stranger talking about Jason's son. The young black woman was too aggressive and Margie took a position of caution.

"I'm not sure if I understand what you're looking for. I have to admit our meeting here like this is rather strange, don't you think?"

"I believe there's a reason for everything. Please help me if you can. I hope I find the child and talk to his handsome father. He is the best lookin' white man I've ever seen."

Margie was becoming more interested in her new acquaintance by the second. "You know Jason?"

"I know him, all right. Jessie brought him to my house before they went away. They stayed the night. And what a night it was. Me and Jessie always shared what we had. That was the last time I saw her." Margie wasn't sure what Ruby meant by her riddle-like information, but she had the idea she didn't like the possibilities. She also knew that nothing involving Jason would surprise her.

"If you are a friend of Jason's you have to take me to him."

"And why must I do that? Is seeing the child your only reason?"

"No, it's not. Jason and his mother are in great danger and I have to warn them. That's the least I can do for Jessie and her baby. The baby doesn't need to lose his daddy too."

"What kind'a danger are you talkin' about?"

"The kind that kills ya."

* * *

Mary C. had dressed and walked out onto her front porch. Hawk was putting up her new wooden bench swing.

"Look at you. You are too good to me. When did you get it?"

Hawk looked up at her from his kneeling position on the porch floor. "I've had it out back for a couple of days. I just didn't have a chance to put it up." Mary C. touched Hawk's face tenderly as they both heard the sound of a car engine approaching from the road. They both turned toward the noise to see Mr. King's white Cadillac hearse driving into the front yard. Jason walked out onto the porch as Mr. King stepped out of his burial wagon. Mary C. moved to the edge of the porch.

"Well now, what brings this world traveler to my house today? Did ya have to come over in that thing?" She motioned to the long hearse parked in her front yard.

"It is merely a mode of transportation, Mary C."

"If you say so, John. Welcome home."

"Thank you. I'm glad to be home." Mr. King moved to the steps of the porch. "Mornin' Hawk. Jason." They both nodded to Mr. King. Mary C. knew John King had something important on his mind. She couldn't recall the last time he was anywhere near her house. She waited for Mr. King to explain his visit. He didn't keep them waiting, but a few seconds.

"I know there's been a great deal of sadness around here. And you three have had much more than folks are supposed to endure. When I went away with Bob and the others I learned of true magic in the world." Hawk stepped to the edge of the porch and stood with Mary C. and Jason. Mr. King went on. "This is gonna sound crazy, but Jason, you have to bring the music box to my house. You all have to come. I'll explain it when you get there with me. Mary C., you know I wouldn't ask you to come if it wasn't important. You'll have to trust me."

* * *

The bell on the door to Miss Margaret's store rang. Peggy turned to see her sister Margie walk through the door followed by the beautiful black woman.

"Peggy, this is Ruby. Ruby, this is my sister, Peggy." Margie walked to the back room of the store. Ruby said, "hey" to Peggy and followed Margie. Peggy had no idea what was going on. Margie closed the door to the back room and they both sat in chairs. Margie spoke first.

"We can talk here and no one will see you or bother us. What do you think is going to happen to Jason and his mother?" Ruby was concerned.

"It would be better for you if you didn't know anything about it. I should tell Jason and let him do what he must." Margie was too curious. Her curiosity had always been her weakness and downfall. She had not learned from her previous mistakes.

"I'll take you to Jason right now, but you have to tell me why."

* * *

Mary C., Jason and Hawk sat in Mr. King's big living room. Billy was lying on the couch next to Mary C. She made sure she did not look at James Thorn's skull sitting above her on the mantle over the fireplace. Mary C. would sit with her back to the awful reminder of one of her evil deeds. The magic music box sat on the table in the middle of the room. Mary C. spoke first.

"I'm not sure what you want here today, John, but this thing here is not a toy to play with."

"I know that, Mary C., Norman told me about it when I was with him two nights ago. He told me Jason had it. He also told me the others didn't know all it could do. Norman was surprised when Bob gave it away. It does much more than give dreams of pleasure. It opens doors to the other worlds. It depends on the setting and the mind set of the individuals involved at the time. Norman said my house was the perfect setting to enter the world beyond us. I only need the carousel to open the door. I want you to allow me to turn it on here today with you all here with me to see if such a thing is possible. I can't think of three people I would rather have here with me than you three. You are strong, brave and have met all that has faced you. I hope you will help me find the courage to step through that door to the other side. I know I'm a strange bird, but we all have our little strangeness and just think what we will see if what Norman says is true." His three guests were quiet after Mr. King's lengthy presentation and request. They had all experienced the carousel. Hawk had to speak.

"I ain't much on all this hocus pocus, but I'll stay with Mary C. if she wants to stay."

Mary C. looked at Mr. King. "John, you really think there's a door here in this house to another world?"

"If it doesn't work we can all laugh about how foolish I was. If it works, who knows what will happen?"

Mary C. looked back at Hawk. "Let's humor the man. I'd like to see what's on the other side myself." Mr. King was surprised when Mary C. reached over to the carousel and pushed the lever to turn it on. The carousel started turning, the music began playing and the lights began bouncing off the walls and ceiling of the large room. The lights flashed in all their eyes as if the music box was in all their heads. Mary C. looked down and saw the lights flashing in Billy's big eyes. In a matter of seconds all four of them saw only the flashing lights. Mary C. turned to the fireplace and saw the lights flashing in the empty eye sockets of James Thorn's skull. She looked away. She could not focus on any of the others in the room. She knew they were sitting with her, she just couldn't see them through the lights. She was afraid.

"Hawk!" There was no answer. "John! Jason!" There was no answer.

Hawk yelled, "Mary C." No answer. Mr. King and Jason said nothing.

The multi-colored lights filled the ceiling above Mary C. It was as if all the lights left the walls and gathered on the ceiling. They moved closer together until they were spinning as one big light. The single light moved down from the ceiling to the floor in the center of the room.

Mary C. heard Elvis singing. It was coming from the

spinning light. She looked down at the bottom of the light and her heart pounded against her rib cage when she saw a pair of black and white be-bop saddle oxford shoes step out of the light. She looked up from the shoes to see her deceased brother, Bobby, step from the light and dance across the floor in front of her. He smiled but wasn't looking at Mary C. as he moved into the next room. Mary C. was frozen with fear where she sat and could not move to follow him, even if she had the courage to do so. Jason saw him, too, but his Uncle Bobby was standing at the wheel of his shrimp boat, Mary C., and Bobby was yelling, "Jetty Man! Jetty Man!" The aroma of Uncle Bobby's favorite Old Spice cologne filled Jason's nostrils. Mr. King did not see Bobby, nor did Hawk

Hawk's blood ran cold when Little Zeke Shackelford, the young man who died from a heart attack after Hawk had hit him, stepped out of the light and stood next to a jukebox. Little Zeke put money into the slot of the jukebox, looked at Hawk and moved back to the light. No one saw Little Zeke but Hawk.

Jason saw Jake, the Mayport Vampire, walk from the light with his black trench coat trailing behind him. Jake still had the rope around his neck that hung him at the oak tree. The skinny black man held a Pepsi Cola in one hand and a roll of cheese and bologna in the other. Jake hurried into the next room and out of Jason's sight. Only Jason saw Jake.

James Thorn stood in front of Mary C. and offered her an easy Black Jack whiskey. She reached for the glass of liquor and it was gone. She looked toward his skull on the mantle, but the darkness covered the room. She looked back at the light and saw James tied to the tree. His eyes screamed for her help. Then Mary C.'s latest victim ran from the light and into the other room. Eve Klim was naked except for the tattoos covering her body. Officer Jimmy Johnston reached with his hand from the light toward Mary C. She did not take his hand as he fell back into the light.

Jason yelled in defiance when Charlie Klim ran from the light and asked Jason for his Derby hat. Jason swung his fist at Charlie, but he was not there. No one else saw Charlie.

Figures began running freely from the light. All of them ran at Mary C. She was able to recognize some of their faces. The black man called Truck, the voodoo queen, Voo Swar, and her old friend, Skinny Shimp, were three she recognized. Mary C. screamed when six Rottweilers ran out of the light and into the living room. The wild pack of dogs jumped on the couch with Mary C.'s grandson. Mary C. could see the spinning carousel through the light as she hit and kicked the dogs. She picked up the music box and threw it at the dogs. The light was gone. There was no music. Mary C. saw Billy on the couch next to her. The carousel was still on the table. It had stopped spinning. Hawk opened his eyes and looked around the room. Jason stood up and walked into the other room. He was looking for his Uncle Bobby. Mr. King opened his eyes and looked at Mary C.

"Well, I guess ol' Norman was wrong. I feel like a fool askin' y'all to do this." He looked at Hawk. "I'm really sorry, Hawk, I was just hopin' it was true. I guess folks are right about me needin' to grow up. Can I get y'all some coffee?"

* * *

Margie was shocked, scared and mesmerized at Ruby's story about the Ax, his dogs and his evil intentions. She knew Mary C. had killed the voodoo queen and four others, so she knew there was a possibility the revenge plot was true. Margie would do anything to protect Mary C., the baby and Jason. She decided to take Ruby to see them.

The ride home from Mr. King's authentic haunted house was without conversation for the three ghost watchers.

Mary C. walked into her house. Jason passed her and carried Billy to his bed. Hawk, finally, had to speak his mind.

"Something happened to me over there, Mary C. I'm not sure what it was and I don't know if it was real or not. I think somethin' happened to you, too. Am I wrong?" Mary C. took a deep breath. "No, you're not wrong. But, I don't think it's somethin' we need to talk about. Okay?"

"Okay." Hawk understood. Mary C. left Hawk in the front room and went to Jason's bedroom where he was sitting on the bed next to Billy. She stood at the door. Jason looked up at his mother and smiled.

"Uncle Bobby looked good, didn't he?" She smiled, too.

"He always did." A knock at the front door interrupted their Uncle Bobby moment. Hawk opened the door to see Margie and Ruby standing on the porch.

"Mr. Hawk, we need to talk to Miss Mary C. and Jason. This is Ruby. She has something you need to know." Hawk looked at Ruby.

"It's true, sir. It is a matter of life and death." Hawk stepped back from the door entrance and allowed the two beauties to enter the house. Mary C. walked from the hallway. Margie saw Mary C.

"Miss Mary C., this is Ruby. She has to talk to you and Jason." Ruby was not an invited guest and she was black. Mary C. was always on guard.

"And what is it that you need to say to me?" Jason walked into the front room. Ruby's face lit up.

"Hey, it's my twistin' buddy. Jason, how are you?" The

voluptuous young black woman hugged Jason like they were long lost friends. The other three looked at Jason with curious eyes. Ruby ended her "Let him feel my breasts, again" hug and stepped back.

"Where's Jessie's baby?"

Mary C. stepped forward. "Wait a second, girl. If you think you're walkin' in here and see that baby, you're wrong."

Jason joined in. "It's all right, mama. She was Jessie's friend.

"Now, the last time you told me it was all right for someone to see Billy, I had to fight for our lives. Did you forget that?" Jason knew his mother was right. Hawk had to add to the situation.

"You said this was a matter of life and death. That was a pretty strong statement for a stranger. You are not seein' that baby after that comment." Margie hoped they would listen to her.

"Miss Mary C., a group of black people are going to try and hurt you and Jason again. Ruby is here to save you from them. She doesn't want Jessie's baby to lose his father or grandmother." Mary C. looked at Ruby, but she talked to Margie.

"You believe her?"

"Yes, ma'am, I do."

CHAPTER TEN

THE MAYPORT SUN WOULD BE GONE WITHIN THE HOUR. THE ARMY of revenge and the devil dogs had gathered in Macadoo's backyard. The Ax was strapping on his six dragon knives as a symbol of his Satanism. He had one strapped to the outside of both legs, one on each side of his waist, one strapped to his forearm and one strapped to his back between his shoulder blades. He looked like a killing machine as he stepped into the group of assembled revenge warriors.

* * *

Ruby sat on Jason's bed holding Billy in her arms. She looked up at Jason standing by the bed. "He's beautiful like you and Jessie. He's got her eyes."

Mary C. couldn't take it. She was worried and disgusted with the beautiful black intruder.

"Tell us something we don't already know." Ruby put Billy back on the bed and turned to the others.

"There is an awful man. He's called the Ax. He's been told all his life that he is the son of the devil and he believes it. He lives it. He has been chosen to punish you and your family for

the death of his mother, the woman called Voo Swar. She raised
him as the devil's son. I know this sounds crazy, but it's true. I
don't know when, but it will be soon. I'm scared to death bein'
here right now. If he finds out I came here he'll kill me, too."

Hawk had a question.

"Why are you doin' this? You could be setting us up."

"But I'm not. I loved Jessie like she was my sister. She loved
Jason. I don't want her child to be without a father. I owe that
to Jessie. She should have never got hooked up with you crazy
white folks, but she did and that baby needs to be safe and
loved as a tribute to her. That's my reason. Take it or leave it.
Think what ya want. I need to get out of here. Me comin' here
was a mistake." She looked at Mary C. "I can see that now. I
really hope you don't all die here tonight." Ruby bent down
and kissed Billy on his little cheek. Then she turned and kissed
Jason on his lips. "I need to get back on the ferry before dark."
She walked to the front of the house. They all followed her.
Margie spoke up.

"I'll walk with you to the ferry slip. If that's okay with
you."

"I'd like that. This ain't been such a friendly place. Thank
you." The two young women walked out onto the front porch.
Ruby looked back at the others.

"He has a pack of wild killer dogs that do his bidding and
he's deep in the evil of voodoo. I thought you should know
that." Margie lifted her hand and waved good-bye to Mary C.
Ruby walked out of Mary C.'s front yard with Margie following behind her. The sun was almost gone from the west side of
the St. Johns River.

*   *   *

The Ax had his canine war party in the back of his black El Camino truck. There were no hunting boxes this time. The dogs were loose in the back bed of the truck. Two cars followed the El Camino as it moved away from Macadoo's house. The sound of the song, "Shotgun", by Junior Walker and the All Stars came out of the Blue Moon Tavern as the three-vehicle war caravan moved past the black honky tonk.

*   *   *

Mary C., Hawk and Jason sat at the kitchen table. Hawk had the lead.

"We need to take this thing seriously just in case she's tellin' the truth. I'm sure there's a lot a voodoo believers around Mayport who would like to get their revenge." Mary C. had to tell what she knew. "She's tellin' the truth." Hawk and Jason looked at Mary C. They were surprised with her comment. "I saw the dogs at John's house. The carousel showed me the dogs. They'll kill Billy if we can't stop 'em."

*   *   *

Macadoo sat alone at her usual table in the Blue Moon Tavern. She watched the handsome and smart Lamar Harris slow dancing with a pretty young girl. She smiled and yelled across the room.

"Don't let that man sweet talk ya, girl. He's good lookin' and smart too, so you be careful." Lamar and the young lady smiled and Lamar danced her toward Macadoo. They moved close to her table. Lamar was interested in the reason for Macadoo's outburst.

"Now why would you want to warn my friend about me? I am quite harmless."

Macadoo shook her head. "You might be a lot of things, but harmless sho' ain't one of 'em." Lamar began to move his dance partner away from the table. Macadoo's words stopped his exit.

"The Ax is here and he will do the deed tonight. It is probably happening as we speak." Lamar stopped and released the young lady.

"Excuse me for a moment." The young woman walked to sit at a bar stool and Lamar walked to Macadoo. "Johnny D. came here for you?" Macadoo smiled and nodded.

"He's here in full force and he has followers. After tonight the evil woman will be gone and all who have suffered at her hands will be avenged. You said to tell you when he was here and when he would face her. The time is here."

The El Camino and the other two cars stopped at a clearing in the woods about a hundred yards away from Mary C.'s back yard. The army didn't know it, but they would take the same attack route the Calypsos had taken the night they all died. The Ax got out of the El Camino. He carried a sawed off shotgun as his ultimate weapon of choice. Each member of the army had a gun of some kind. They were prepared to rid the Mayport fishing village of the woman known as Mary C.

* * *

Hawk threw a shotgun to Jason and a box of shells. Mary C. took her shotgun from behind the door and pulled the pump handle down, chambering a shell. Hawk watched her as she put the gun on the bed and picked up Billy. She placed the child on a pillow and pushed him under the bed. The oak baby had been under a bed before. She talked to her grandson.

"I probably should have asked Margie to take you with her, but I know no one will protect you like me. I love you." Mary C. positioned herself on the floor next to the window in Jason's bedroom. It was the best place to see into the back yard. She looked up and saw that Hawk was still standing at the bedroom door.

"I'll be fine. You just don't let 'em get this far." Hawk took a deep breath and moved down the hall. He knew Mary C. was a rare breed of woman.

* * *

The Ax stood with his small army. The devil dogs were still in the back of the truck, sensing the hunt. One of the men opened the trunk of one of the cars. He took out a box, reached in and began handing out whiskey bottles filled with gasoline with a rag plugged into the top of each bottle. The criminal world called them Molotov Cocktails. The blacks of Mayport called them Klan Cookers. Each soldier would carry one into battle.

* * *

Margie had taken Ruby to her house and had called Mr. Butler at the police station. She told him Ruby's story about the possible attack on Mary C. Margie hung up the phone and turned to Ruby.

"The police will be here soon. You did the right thing."

Ruby nodded. "I want to catch the next ferry. I'm really scared."

Mr. Butler held the radio microphone to his face. "Paul, David, you out there?"

"This is David, sir. Paul's here with me."

"Get out to Mayport and go to Mary C.'s house. Jimmy's

girlfriend just called me and she and some other young woman think there's gonna be somethin' bad happenin' out there. Check it out and let me know when you get there."

"We're on our way, sir." They were twenty minutes away from Mayport and moving. They had no idea they would be too late. Ruby was on the ferry and headed back to Cosmos. Hawk and Jason joined Mary C. in Jason's bedroom. Hawk looked at Mary C. He knew she was prepared to fight.

"You all right?"

"I'm fine and I'm stayin' here with y'all. You think they're comin'?"

"I don't know. I don't know what to think." Jason looked at the empty bed. Mary C. pointed under the bed. Jason smiled. Mary C. looked out the window. Hawk saw her eyes change.

"Oh my God. They're comin'." Hawk and Jason moved to the window to see dark figures walking out of the woods behind the house. They were spread out across the back yard and it was obvious they were armed. Hawk cocked his Winchester thirty- ought-six rifle and moved to the back door of the house. Jason moved to the front door and Mary C. stayed next to the window. There were no lights on in the house. Hawk had already made sure of that. He lay on the floor behind the back door and drew a bead with his rifle sights on the lead intruder.

The attacker lit the rag of his Klan Cooker and lifted it above his head to throw the gas bomb at the house. Hawk fired the first shot of the night. The bullet shattered the whiskey bottle full of gasoline before it left the man's hand. The gas ignited and engulfed him in flames. The war with the devil's son had begun.

The burning man fell to his knees screaming in fear and

pain. Three more men lit their homemade bombs and threw them at the house. One hit the porch sending fiery gas against the porch wall. Another fell on the roof and fire spread over the back bedroom. The third bomb fell on the ground next to the house, but gas splashed on the wall and the flames crawled up the side of the house. The last two cookers hit the porch like the first one. Mary C's house was on fire. Hawk knew they would not be able to enter through the back door while the fire was blazing. He moved to the bedroom with Mary C.

"We gotta get you two out of here. I don't want to lose y'all." Hawk looked out the window to see how far the attackers had advanced. He had to look a second time to be sure he saw what he thought he saw. The fire lit up the back yard. One of the attackers fell to the ground as a figure moving in the dark went by him. Hawk saw a flash in the air and another man fell to his knees and then face down on the ground. This time Hawk was able to see the reason for the fallen enemies. He saw Sandeep Singh pull the Kirpan sword from the back of the man on the ground and move back into the darkness. The Punjabi priest and warrior had returned to protect the golden child once again. Hawk yelled to Jason.

"Jason, get Billy and your mother to the front room. I'll tell you when to get out." Hawk gave Mary C. his rifle and he took the pump action shotgun. "Go up front." Hawk walked to the burning end of the house. He knew they would not expect him to come out that way through the flames. He took a running start and jumped through the flames that covered the back door. He didn't fire the shotgun until he landed in the yard. His first shot hit another assassin dead center in the chest. Hawk turned quickly to see Sandeep slit the throat of another. Hawk saw the last man of the six attackers run back toward the woods. A gunshot rang out as the Ax shot the

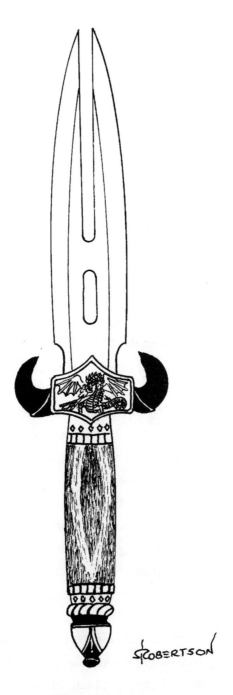

Dragon Knife

retreating soldier. There was an evil silence in the back yard as the six intruders lay dead.

The Ax stepped out of the woods and stood there, scanning the battlefield. Sandeep stepped toward him, bowed and lifted the Kirpan over his head. The Ax smiled, dropped his gun on the ground and pulled two of the dragon knives out of his belt. He held them high over his head. Hawk lifted his gun, but the Ax was too far away for the shotgun pellets to reach him. He had given Mary C. the rifle. Mary C. watched from the bedroom window. She knew Sandeep had returned to save the child.

Sandeep ran toward the Ax with the Kirpan held high. The Ax threw one of the dragon knives at the charging Sandeep, but the Punjabi warrior was too quick and agile. He dodged it easily. Sandeep blocked the second knife with the Kirpan as he drew closer to the devil. The Ax lifted his hands over his head and yelled "Abaddon."

Sandeep swung the Kirpan at the Ax's head. The devil man was quick, too, and he moved to the side causing the Punjabi to miss on his first pass. Sandeep steadied himself and turned to do battle with the Ax. The Ax smiled as the six devil dogs came running out of the woods directly behind Sandeep, led by the massive hellhound, Abaddon. The Punjabi turned to see teeth and eyes coming out of the darkness. He only had time to swing the Kirpan one time before the dogs slammed into him and took him down to the ground. His one thrust of the sword cut off Shedim's hind legs. The legless dog yelped in pain from the deep and clean slice of the Kirpan.

The other five dogs knocked Sandeep off his feet and took him down again. He could not fight as the dogs sunk their teeth deep into his arms, throat and legs. He did manage to stick Calabim in the stomach at close range with the Kirpan, but the dog continued the attack. Sandeep knew the Ax was standing there watching the vicious attack. The Punjabi knew he was going to die. He found one last moment of strength and threw the holy Kirpan at the Ax. The devil man only saw the flash of the moving blade a second before the long moon-curved blade sunk deep into the evil one's groin. The Ax fell to the ground in shock and pain as the devil dogs tore the Punjabi priest to pieces.

Hawk knew he could not help the priest. He ran around the house to the front door. He entered to find Mary C., Billy and Jason waiting for his directions.

"You can't leave yet. The dogs are out there. He's here, too. Give me the rifle." Mary C. traded guns with Hawk again. "Mary C., the fire won't get this far for a while. Me and Jason's gotta kill the dogs. I don't think they'll stop even if we do kill this man. The priest hurt him with that big knife. We gotta kill the dogs first. Don't shoot unless they're close. We'll be back. " Jason followed Hawk out the front door. They moved together slowly along the side of the house. Hawk looked out toward the place where the Ax had stood. He saw what was left of Sandeep and the hind legless dog. The Ax and the other dogs were gone. The back of the house was blazing. Hawk turned to Jason.

"Check the other side of the house and then go back up front. Stay with your mama. He's still out here. I can feel him and the damn dogs. Wait as long as you can before you take them into the yard." Jason looked down at the burning body of the first casualty as he moved away from Hawk.

Hawk held up his rifle and walked toward Sandeep's body. The back yard had the other bodies on the ground every few steps. He watched the woods as he knelt down on one knee next to the dead priest. There was a noise in the air behind

Hawk, but he had no time to turn before the split blade of a dragon knife sunk deep into his shoulder blades at the base of his neck. He knew the point of the blade had emerged through his skin in the front of his throat. Hawk reached for the blade as he stood up and turned to face the Ax.

The devil's son threw another dragon knife and the blade went into Hawk's chest directly above his heart. The five remaining devil dogs, including Calabim, the one Sandeep had stabbed, did not make a sound as they ran past Hawk toward the house. The Ax stepped out of the darkness of the woods. His pants were covered in his own blood from the blade of the Kirpan. Hawk was in too much shock and pain to notice the serious injury to his enemy. The Ax was only a few feet away from the dying Lester Hawkins.

"I can't believe you're still standin', mister. They said she had her own protectors and they were right. You know those dogs are eatin' her and that baby right now, don't ya?" Hawk couldn't move or respond. He just stared at the devil.

Mary C. had moved Billy to the front door so she could wait until the last second to run. She covered him with a pillow and stood up to look outside. A noise down the hall made her turn to see two of the dogs, Djinn and Habbalah, coming through the fire at the back door. She lifted the shotgun and pulled the trigger as Habbalah jumped into the air toward her. The gun exploded and so did the dog's head when the pellets hit it at a five-inch range. The second dog, Djinn, hit Mary C. like a runaway train, knocking her out of the front door and onto the porch. She rolled away as the dog grabbed her ankle with his teeth. Mary C. kicked wildly at the dog's huge head. A gunshot blasted and the dog released its death grip. Mary C. rolled away even more. She looked up to see Jason standing near her. He had killed the dog.

Mary C. jumped up and ran back into the house for Billy. Jason stood on the porch. He saw two more dogs running toward him. Jason didn't know it, but he would soon meet Lilin and Calabim. Jason turned to run into the burning house. He stopped when he saw his mother standing at the door with her shotgun raised and pointed at the approaching devil dogs. Jason turned to face the charging dogs. He was side by side with his mother when he lifted his gun. The two bloodthirsty Rottweilers ran up the porch steps. Mary C. and Jason pulled the triggers of their guns at the same time, dropping both devil dogs at their feet. Mary C.'s eyes lit up when Hawk walked around the corner of the house. He moved slowly. Jason stepped out of the house holding Billy. He looked toward Hawk.

"We need to get mama and Billy away from here." Hawk didn't respond. He walked to the steps and dropped to his knees and then to his back on the ground. Mary C. could see the dragon knives sticking out of his chest and the blood flowing from the front of his throat. She moved down the steps and knelt down next to him. She knew he was dead. Mary C. stood up and turned to Jason.

"Take Billy to Miss Margaret's house."

"You come with us."

"I ain't leavin' Hawk. Ain't no dogs gonna eat him. Get Billy out of here. Do what I tell ya." She turned to her blazing house. "Look what they did to my house. Now, go on like I said." Jason moved to Hawk's truck and put Billy on the seat. He looked back as his mother knelt down next to Hawk. Jason stomped on the gas pedal, spinning the truck wheels in the dirt and drove the truck out of the front yard.

Mary C. reached down and pulled the knife out of Hawk's chest and tossed it on the ground away from her. She didn't change her facial expression as she turned his head and pulled the other knife out of the back of his neck. She dropped it on the ground as soon as it came out. Mary C. touched Hawk's cheek holding her hand on him for a few seconds and then stood up. She picked up her shotgun, pulled the pump handle down and chambered a shell. She heard the scream of a police siren in the distance. Officer David Boos drove his police car past the little jetties with his partner, Paul Short next to him. They were headed to Mary C.'s burning house and the Mayport war zone.

Mary C. stood in her back yard with her shotgun at her hip in the firing position. Her eyes widened when she saw the number of bodies around her. She looked toward the woods. She felt his presence.

"You still here, ain't ya?" She walked past Sandeep's body, but didn't take her eyes off the woods. "Devil got your tongue?" She walked to the edge of the woods. "Ain't it funny how we feel each other? That priest man hurt ya bad with that big knife, didn't he?" Mary C. heard a painful moan to her right and she stopped to look in that direction. Her eyes widened again when she saw the Ax sitting up with his back against the trunk of a small tree.

"There you are." He was covered in blood from his wound. The holy Kirpan remained deep in his groin area. He held another dragon knife in one hand and the handle of the Kirpan in his other hand. The devil had no strength to throw the dragon knife at Mary C. as she stood above him. "You can't get that thing out, can ya?"

His eyes were wide open with pain and disbelief. He swallowed, took one of his last deep breaths and whispered in his raspy voice.

"Abaddon." Mary C. saw the huge mutant dog walk out of the woods behind his master. She raised the shotgun and took aim at the monster Rottweiler. The Ax whispered again. "You cannot hurt us. My father will not allow it." Abaddon's eyes were locked on Mary C.'s eyes. He did not move toward her. She held the gun to her shoulder as the devil dog walked back into the dark woods. The Ax watched his destroyer disappear into the night. He turned to face Mary C. and her shotgun.

"Your protectors have saved you once again. Why does my father allow you to remain? How many will die before your curse ends?"

Mary C. raised the shotgun. "At least one more." She pulled the trigger.

* * *

The flashing lights of a police car bounced off the front of Mary C.'s burning house. Lamar Harris stood next to his car on the road leading to Mary C.'s house as a police car drove past him and stopped in the front yard. He had seen nothing of the battle and could only see the burning house. A fire truck rolled in behind the police car, but they were way too late.

Officers David Boos and Paul Short jumped out of the car, drew their guns and moved cautiously across the front yard. The house was in full blaze in front of them. The two police officers would find the dead bodies of Johnny D. Bryant, Sandeep Singh, six other men, five devil dogs and the Hawk, Lester Hawkins. They would not find the huge devil dog, Abaddon or Mary C.